Lowlander Silverback

Lowlander Silverback
ISBN-13: 978-1517421229
ISBN-10: 1517421225
Copyright © 2015, T. S. Joyce
First electronic publication: September 2015

T. S. Joyce
www.tsjoycewrites.wordpress.com

All Rights Are Reserved. No part of this book may be used or reproduced in any manner whatsoever without written permission, except in the case of brief quotations embodied in critical articles and reviews. The unauthorized reproduction or distribution of this copyrighted work is illegal. No part of this book may be scanned, uploaded or distributed via the Internet or any other means, electronic or print, without the author's permission.

NOTE FROM THE AUTHOR:
This book is a work of fiction. The names, characters, places, and incidents are products of the writer's imagination or have been used fictitiously and are not to be construed as real. Any resemblance to persons, living or dead, actual events, locale or organizations is entirely coincidental. The author does not have any control over and does not assume any responsibility for third-party websites or their content.

Published in the United States of America

First digital publication: September 2015
First print publication: September 2015

Lowlander Silverback

(Gray Back Bears, Book 5)

T. S. Joyce

ONE

Layla Taylor put on an extra layer of pink lip gloss using the fold-down mirror in her old Civic. She fidgeted with her black tank top with the red and orange lettering of Sammy's Bar and let off a long sigh.

She could do this. She saw him every weekend at the bar, and this was no different.

Scrunching up her nose, she flipped the mirror up and sank into the cushion of her seat. Aw, who was she kidding? Sure, Kong's eyes followed her around the bar when he was there, but he hadn't ever given her the time of day. Hell, sometimes he was downright rude to her, so why was she all fluttery over a man like him? Mac had taught her more self-respect than to chase a man who didn't want to be chased.

Of course, Kong probably didn't know he

was being chased because...well...she sucked at chasing. Her game with men wasn't awesome, which was ridiculous since she was a bartender. She talked to people for a living and could be charming when she wanted to, but when it came to Kong, she turned into a complete mouse.

Her cheeks heated just thinking about the last time she'd tried to talk to him. It hadn't gone well. She'd only found her bravery that night because while she'd worked her shifts, Kong had watched her constantly with something akin to hunger in his eyes, but when she'd approached, he'd shut her down immediately.

But there was something about the way he watched her that she found so attractive. Alluring even. Unless she was reading him completely wrong, the intensity of his gaze said he wanted her on some base level, but he hadn't acted on it for three years. His silent attention was such a turn-on and now the strength of the build-up had turned monumental. For her at least, because again, Kong was completely indifferent when she tried to start up conversations with him. The man was an enigma.

The little green numbers turned to 8:00 on

the dash clock, so she pushed open her creaky door with the toe of her black boot and unfolded from her car. After straightening her ripped-up dark-wash jeans, she pulled the hem of her tank top until her girls peeked out just enough. Those were her real "tip getters." And she needed lots of those tonight. Bills were piling up, and Mac was depending on her.

She strode across the gravel parking lot and pushed open the back door.

"Hey, there she is," Jake said. At five-foot-four with an easy smile and one helluva beard, he gestured her toward his office.

Jake was the new owner of Sammy's, and he'd only been running the place for the past six months, but Layla liked him fine. He'd changed a few things in the transition, but the big stuff was still the same. Like the Beck Brothers playing every weekend and Beer Pong Tuesdays. He was even sponsoring a booth at the Lumberjack Wars in a few weeks.

She ducked into his dim office and tried not to stare at the signed pictures of registered shifters on the wall as she tucked her purse into the bottom drawer of his desk. He was also a shameless shifter groupie, which was why he'd moved to Saratoga and bought

Sammy's in the first place.

"Okay, I'm toying around with a new idea," he said excitedly. "Tell me what you think."

Jake pushed a stack of multi-colored flyers toward her, and she picked up the neon orange one off the top. Front and center was a big, burly man in plaid chugging a beer, shirt sleeves rolled up to show muscular forearms. On either side of him were two fearsome grizzlies. *Shifter Night, when single bears drink free*, the flyer read in arching bubble letters across the top.

Layla's eyes went wide. "Uh, Jake, you know how much one of those boys can drink, right? Copious amounts of beer. Gallons." She could almost hear money flying out of the register.

"Yes, but the Boarlanders are the only singles left, and I think it would be worth it to attract more shifter groupies to the bar. They make up the bulk of our income now, Layla. Think about it. It'll be the opposite of Ladies Night. If we do it every week, say on Thursday or Friday, shifter groupies will be lining up out the door if they know the single bears will be coming in. It won't be the hit or miss that it usually is with disappointed tourists not getting a glimpse of the tail-chasin' shifters when they show up on the wrong night."

"Okay." Layla nodded, seeing the merit in his idea. "The Boarlanders aren't the only single crew left, though. What about Kong and his two guys?" Because they were definitely single. She'd checked for rings, and they didn't entertain human ladies much.

"Oh, I don't think Kong is a bear."

"Wait, what?" she asked, her eyes drifting to the picture of Kong and his crew that was nailed to the wall behind Jake's desk. "Of course he is. I've seen his eyes glow bright green, and he's the size of a small shrimping vessel."

"I didn't say he wasn't a shifter, just that I don't think he's a bear like the others. Why wouldn't he have registered with the rest of them?"

Layla shrugged. "I don't know. Lots of reasons. For example, the government is full of shit for making them register in the first place, and maybe it's his way of saying 'Damn the man.'"

"You ever heard him growl like the others?"

That drew her up short. She sank onto the cracked leather office chair and shook her head. Nope. Never. Huh. She'd thought she was crushing hard on a grizzly shifter all this time, but perhaps Jake was right. The mysteries surrounding Kong grew by another layer as she lifted her gaze to his picture again. In it, he was sitting between his two crew members, eyes dead-looking. Jake's relentless autograph-seeking did that to some of the dominant ones. Pissed them off. Not that Jake noticed or cared. Kong's angry photo with his crew was one of Jake's favorites, as highlighted by the prime spot on his wall. Right under a single spotlight, front and center.

"All right, so will you include Kong's crew on Shifter Night?"

"Not until he registers. Or no! Not until he pulls his weight and fucks a couple of groupies."

"Jake!"

"What? They are the honey attracting the bees, Layla. And from what I've seen, Kong hasn't taken a single girl home. When he dips his toe into helping me bring in customers, he can have all the free booze he wants. Oh! Could you tell him that? Here." Jake ripped bright pink and neon green flyers off the top of the stack and shoved them into her hands with the one she already held. "Tell his crew our plans and explain why they need to get their dicks wet."

"Oh my gosh, Jake, no." Layla shook her head and headed for the door, clutching the flyers. "If they aren't chasing women, it's because they don't want wives or mates or whatever they call it when they pair up." And she wasn't encouraging Kong to screw groupies, nope, nope, nope.

"I'll give you twenty bucks on top of your tips tonight."

Layla halted her retreat, her back to him. Double damn, she'd almost made it to the door.

"I know you need the money for Mac. Just talk to them subtly, explain there's free weekly booze in it for them, and let them make the decision to participate on their own. You don't even have to do a hard sell. I mean, shit, it's free booze and pussy. What are they going to say? No?" Jake let off a single, loud laugh.

"Why can't *you* talk to them about it?" she asked, turning slowly.

"Because I don't have those." He looked pointedly at her boobs and arched his eyebrows. "They'll listen to you over me any day. Thirty bucks."

Layla let off a growl and muttered, "Fine.

Thirty bucks."

The nerves hit in the hallway. She was going to talk to Kong, on purpose. And not just to get his drink order. She pressed her back against the wood paneling in the hallway and closed her eyes tightly. Gah, she was an easy mark. All Jake had to do was wave a few ten dollar bills in her face and she was asking how high he wanted her to jump. Her self-respect was swirling the toilet right now.

Pursing her lips, Layla pushed off the wall and strode into the main room of Sammy's, her boots making sticky sounds across the floor. She mopped the damned thing every night, but the townies couldn't seem to go ten minutes without party-fouling and sloshing their drinks everywhere.

As she made her way behind the bar, she smiled politely at Jackson, who untied his apron and shoved a wad of tips in his pocket as he passed. It looked like mostly one dollar bills, which meant the mid-day shift must've been slow. One look behind the bar, and she puffed air out her cheeks and tried to figure out where to begin. Jackson was nice and was good with the customers, but holy moose patties, he was the biggest slob she'd ever encountered. Maybe all bachelors were like that. No, Mac had never been a slob, and his wife had died years ago. Perhaps it was different with widowers than bachelors, though.

"Hellooo," Barney sang out. "I've been waiting ten minutes for you to come and refill my drink."

Barney was a regular, and he was also a steady source of headache material. Lucky for him, she was a pro. "Why didn't you have Jackson refill you, Barney?"

"Because," he slurred as she refilled his whiskey and coke, "Jackson don't do nothin' for my boner."

"Charming. There you go. Just give me a holler when you need another. You want me to turn the volume up?" She pointed to the television above the bar and waited with the sweetest smile she could manage over her gritted teeth. Barney liked sports, and turning up the volume was the quickest way to get his attention off her.

He slurped and nodded, then pulled a bowl of mixed nuts to his chest and began snacking while she searched for the remote. Freaking Jackson. Empty bottles, dirty rags, bottle caps, and used wine glasses littered the bar. She was a tidy person by nature, and cleaning up after

Jackson's shift was her least favorite chore. She turned to Barney who was staring at her tits with a gap-toothed grin. Well, it was one of her least favorite. Barney tipped her well, though, so he could stare all he wanted. This was part of the job. She'd known it the day she was hired a few years ago. Did she like being ogled by handsy strangers? No. But she had a steady job in a small town with a nice enough boss, and the tips kept food on the table. She was lucky to work here, a mantra she would probably repeat to herself a hundred times tonight.

Saturdays were busy thanks to the two men sauntering in through the front door right now. Denison and Brighton Beck, and she had a genuine smile for those boys. Denison waved as he set his guitar case up on the stage.

"Let me clean up, and I'll get you two a drink," she called across the bar.

"No rush. I know Jackson's shite at cleaning up his mess," Denison said through a grin.

He and his brother had been playing here on the weekends as long as she'd worked here. They were the reason she hadn't felt frightened like some of the other people in town when the bear shifters of Saratoga had begun registering to the public. Denison and Brighton were always nice to her. Growly as hell if anyone pissed them off, and sure, they could rip someone's esophagus through their mouth hole if they were ever so inclined, but the twins had a strong moral compass, and damn they could sing. Or, at least Denison could. His brother, Brighton, had no voice. Didn't stop him from the raspy whisper he used in the microphone, but Brighton shredded guitar in the background while Denison sang lead. And shit could they play. If they'd had a mind to, they could be big. She'd asked them once why they hadn't gone to Nashville and chased the big stage, but Denison said his inner animal wouldn't let him, and he was happy to stay here where he knew the crowd.

The Becks tuned their guitars and did a sound check while she rushed to clean up the bar to shining. And every few minutes, her eyes lifted to the door to check for Kong. An irritating habit, but she couldn't help herself and had stopped trying weeks ago when her crush had gotten bigger.

Bar cleaned and a few drink orders refilled, she strode to the stage with a couple of light beers in glass mugs. "Are Everly and

Danielle coming tonight?" she asked.

Denison shook his head as he took the drinks from her hand and set them on stools beside him and Brighton's chairs. "Not tonight."

"Oh, man. I was looking forward to seeing them. It's been a couple of weeks."

"Everly isn't feeling well," Brighton said in that raspy whisper of his.

"She's sick? Oh no! You want me to get Nate to whip up some of his noodle soup? He could have it done by the time y'all finish your last set, and you can take it home to Everly."

"It ain't that kind of sick," Brighton whispered with an arch to his dark eyebrow.

Layla's face went slack, and she stepped closer. "Is she pregnant?"

A grin busted up Brighton's face, and he nodded.

Layla squeaked and hugged his neck. "You're not joking. You wouldn't do that to me. She's pregnant? Holy shit!" Dang, she was getting all misty-eyed. Brighton and his mate had been trying for a baby for a while. "I'm so happy for you. She got any cravings? I'll get Nate on it."

Brighton laughed silently and released her from his hug. "Not yet."

"She's sick as all get out, barfing all the time," Denison said. "I feel bad for her. Danielle's been staying with her while we're up on the landing, and she's taking care of her tonight while we play."

"Aw, poor Ev. Well, if there is anything I can do, you let me know. And Brighton," she murmured, gripping his arm, "congratulations."

"Thanks, Layla," he whispered through a proud grin.

"You boys let me know when you need another drink. Are you eating here tonight?"

"Maybe after the set, before we hit the road."

"Great, just give me a heads up on your second to last song. I'll get Nate on your regular."

"You got it," Denison said distractedly as he threaded a cable from one of the amps to his guitar.

Beaming with happiness, she turned and ran into a solid wall of muscle. Her face smacked right into a big, steely torso. "Shoot," she said in a rush. "I'm sorry. I should've watched where I was..." She arched her neck back and looked directly into the sexy face of Kong. "...walking."

He stared at her passively. Dark eyes steady, cheekbones sharp as ever, and those sexy lips that lifted easily into a smile for everyone but her. He stood straighter with an irritated sigh and clasped his hands behind his back. "It's fine."

"Hi," she said lamely.

He took a step back and angled his face away, eyes never leaving her. His gaze dipped once to her chest, then back to her face, but he didn't respond to her greeting. She was supposed to do something with Kong. Think! Talk to him about something. Her head was spinning from being so close to him. He was tall and strong with wide shoulders and arms that stretched the thin material of his black V-neck T-shirt. A curl of ink peeked out from under the sleeve. She wanted to lick him. Lick him. Shit. Flyer! "I need to talk to you about something."

A single eyebrow arched even higher. Why did he only ever look annoyed around her? "About what?"

"Kong," one of his crew members barked out from the corner.

The behemoth slid an agitated glance over his shoulder, then back to her. "Sorry, not interested in anything you have to say."

"Pussy!" Layla clapped her hand over her mouth as her cheeks lit on fire.

"What?" Kong asked in a low rumble.

"I want to talk to you about pussy." And now she also wanted to melt into the cracks between the floorboards beneath her shoes and possibly die.

His eyes dipped to her boobs again, but when he lifted his gaze to her face, he looked pissed. "Not. Interested."

He turned and walked away, his work boots making hollow sounds across the floor as he strode away from her.

"Oh, my gosh," she whispered, mortified as she escaped to the bar. Other than to take drink orders, she'd never talked to him for that long, and her first sentence involved the word *pussy*? Really? She wanted to curl into a ball under the sink behind the bar.

"Thirty bucks," Jake sang as he poured a wells beer into a tall glass.

From their table, one of Kong's crew lifted his hand to flag her down, and she bit back the urge to beg Jake to serve their table tonight. Because really, this couldn't get any worse. But she grabbed the crumpled flyers and made her way back to their table. Kong suddenly looked really interested in Brighton and Denison's sound check.

A blond man with bright blue eyes ordered them a round of beers. "Do you need to write this down?" he asked when she stood there nodding.

Narrowing her eyes at his rude ass, she said, "I think I can remember three beers." She slapped the flyers down on the table. "My boss wants me to talk to you about Shifter Night at Sammy's. We're going to do it on either Thursday or Friday every week, and shifters will be able to drink free—"

"We ain't shifters," Blondie said through an empty smile.

Her eyes lingered on Kong, who was now frowning down at a napkin he was shredding. With a sigh, she said, "Be that as it may, *if* you were shifters and *if* you showed some interest in the shifter groupies around here, you would be able to drink for free on those nights."

"You mean," Kong said, lifting one of the flyers, "if we fuck groupies, we can drink for free?"

"Yes." Her voice cracked on the word, so she cleared her throat and tried again. "Yes. Or not f-fucked exactly, but maybe an occasional finger bang or make-out session or give some tourist a hickey or even flirted or...something."

"Hard pass," Blondie said, his eyes narrowed to dangerous-looking slits as he shoved the flyers back to her. "We don't stick our dicks in *humans*." The way he said the last word was like a curse.

"But you aren't shifters," she said sarcastically, anger blasting up her spine.

"You stupid bitch. Shut your fucking mouth and bring us our drinks!" Blondie yelled, slamming his palm against the table.

She jumped, and the bar grew quiet. Kong's eyes tightened as he leveled the blond-haired man with a look that raised chills up her arms. "Rhett, enough."

She swallowed hard and picked up the flyers. "It wasn't my idea." She apologized before she turned and jogged back to the bar, hoping her stupid tears would stay in her eyes until then. "I'm taking a break," she gritted out to Jake as she passed.

"Sorry!" her boss called out as she flew down the hallway toward his office.

Such bull crap. That guy, Rhett, didn't have to be so rude. They were always mean to her for some reason she couldn't understand. Short and clipped when they ordered their drinks, but when they talked to other people in the bar, they were sweet as punch, laughing and joking. She didn't get it. Was it because she was human?

She tried to close the office door, but the foundation of Sammy's wasn't great, and the door was now off kilter by half an inch. It creaked back open as she hid in the corner beside the filing cabinet. She hated being talked down to like that. It wasn't like this was a bar full of strangers. Rhett had embarrassed her in front of regulars and in front of the Beck Brothers. In front of her boss! She was trying to keep everything together in her personal life, and her one respite from the poop storm she was dealing with at home was this job where she could turn her mind off and just work. But being called names and getting publicly berated was just another hurt on top of a pile of shit right now.

Her phone rang from her purse, but she ignored it. It was probably another scam call. Hardly anyone had her number. She drew her knees up to her chest and rested her chin on them, staring at the wood grain of the wall. Her phone rang again, and she frowned. Two calls in a row was signature Mac. She scrambled for the drawer with her purse, dug out her cell phone, and accepted the call as fast as she could.

"Hello? Mac, are you okay?"

"Layla? Honey, I got a call earlier from one of the neighbors. She said there's an eviction notice on the front door."

Layla scooted back into her corner and shook her head in disbelief. "That can't be. I just talked to the bank on Monday, and they said they were going to work with us. I got us an extension."

"They're going to take my home."

"No. Mac, this has to be a mix-up or misunderstanding. I'll go by after work and read the notice, and then I'll come by and see you in the morning. I'll bring you breakfast. What's tomorrow? Breakfast casserole day? Gross. I'll bring you bacon and those cheesy eggs you like. And we'll figure this all out. I'll call the bank, too. Mac, I won't let you lose your home. I swear it."

Over her cold and lifeless body was anyone going to take anything else away from the man who'd cared for her all these years.

"I got another check in the mail. Will that help?"

"Yes, of course it will. I'll deposit it before my shift tomorrow, and I'll make a house payment online, okay? We'll figure this out. Stop worrying. Let me do that. You just focus on getting better. I need my scrabble partner back."

Mac chuckled, but it turned into a fit of coughing. "Layla, honey," he wheezed out when he could. "It's okay if we lose it."

"Mac, we won't. I promise. I'm at work making us more money to pay the bank right now."

"Okay, honey. I'll see you in the morning. Extra crispy."

Layla smiled emotionally. "Extra crispy bacon. I'd never forget."

With another layer of stress added to her shoulders, she hung up and muttered a curse. Stupid bank had promised to work with her, especially since she was trying to make up for missed payments. But juggling Mac's hospice bills from Tender Care and her own rent and the mortgage payments on the old house he'd shared with his late wife, she was falling behind on everything. *Failing* at everything.

A tear slipped to her cheek, and she wiped it off with her knuckles.

"I came to apologize for my crew's behavior," Kong said.

A scream clawed its way up the back of her throat as she startled hard against the space she'd shoved herself into. "Geez," she said, clutching her chest, "I didn't see you there."

Kong was leaning on the desk, arms locked and triceps flexed as he gripped the edge of the dinged-up oak. "You can't talk to me anymore."

Layla pulled her knees back up to her chest, squeezed her eyes tightly closed and nodded. This day just kept getting better and better. "Great. Hint taken."

Kong's dark eyes drifted to the door, and he lowered his voice. "It's not safe."

She jerked her gaze to his. "What?"

He shot her a warning look. "Don't approach me anymore. Never again."

She wiped another tear and nodded her head. "Okay."

Kong pushed off the desk to leave but turned and strode to her instead, blocking her into the corner. He yanked her arm until she was standing and pulled her against him. He hugged her so hard, her breath left her. "I'm sorry about whatever is happening. When you were on the phone, I heard... I'm sorry." His hands gripped her hair too tight before he released her. His dark gaze dropped to the floor, and he looked sick when he repeated, "Never again."

Then he strode out of the office, leaving

Layla staring after him and wondering if she'd just dreamed what had happened here.

TWO

Kong clenched his fists and barely avoided slamming the door to the office as he blasted out into the hallway. He could kill Rhett for talking to Layla like that. Damn it all, he wished he could kill both him and Kirk. The punishment would be death, though, or he would've challenged both of them and ended this shit years ago.

"Where did you go?" Rhett asked from the mouth of the hallway. His blue eyes were narrowed in an accusatory glare.

Kong knocked against his shoulder as he passed him. "To apologize to the lady you just verbally maimed in front of everyone."

"She isn't yours to protect, Kong."

"No shit," Kong growled out, turning and slamming him against the wall. He pressed his forearm against Rhett's neck and wanted to choke the life out of the prick. "I never said she was. You can't act like that here. This isn't the family group where you can just talk down to whoever you want. It's a bar full of humans. You'll expose us and worse. She isn't your submissive, you fucking dick." Kong released his throat and pushed off him.

"Fiona will hear about this."

"Great. Tell her I had to smooth over your actions, yet again. I'm sure she'll love to hear you snitch for the billionth time, Rat."

"It's Rhett, and I ain't no snitch. It's my job to make sure you keep your focus."

"Snitching is your job, Rhett. Don't twist it around in your head to make what you do noble."

"You know, you should be thanking me. You could have way worse guards than me and Kirk."

Guards. That word made him want to punch gaping holes through the sheetrock. Everyone had it wrong about the Lowlanders. Rhett and Kirk weren't his crew. They were his handlers, controlling every move he made.

"Look, you were the one who wanted to leave Oregon," Rhett said low. "I get it. A dominant silverback like you needs to roam until he's called to rule the family group. But you decided to live in this shithole town, Kong. Not me and not Kirk."

"Then leave," Kong said through an empty smile. "What's stopping you?"

"Duty. Fiona and the girls don't deserve tainted seed. You signed the abstinence contract—"

"Was forced to sign it—"

"You signed it, and you'll uphold your duty. And what are you fucking complaining about, man? Any male would give their left nut to be in your position. When Fiona calls for you, you're going to be the highest ranking silverback in the world. In the *world*. Fucking King Kong." Rhett shook his head and laughed a humorless sound. "You get to breed the females. All you'll have to do is eat and sleep and make babies and fight. What else could you possibly want out of life?"

Layla.

Kong shook his head and left the hallway. Trying to explain his desire for a single mate to Rhett was pointless. The guard was born a diehard gorilla shifter, drinking the same shit punch the family groups fed all their young. Kong wanted more, though. He wanted to *feel*. He wanted it to matter when he bedded a woman. He didn't want to bounce from bed to bed for the sheer goal of getting the females pregnant. Did he want kids? Hell yeah. He wanted a little baby so bad he stayed up nights thinking about it. He wanted a family of his own more than anything. It was natural for a mature silverback to crave that. But he didn't want a bunch of kids he wasn't allowed to co-parent with their mothers.

For the millionth time, he wished he'd been born a bear shifter. They were his friends. He had watched the Ashe Crew and the Gray Backs with their mates, and he wanted that badly.

At least if he'd been born a bear shifter, he could choose his mate.

But the dominant gorilla inside of him and the birthmark on his back had dictated his destiny from infancy.

What else could he possibly want from life? To have a conversation with an unclaimed woman without catching shit from his crew. To take Layla on a date instead of just watching her when his crew wasn't looking. To kiss her, and hug her when she was crying. To help her through whatever awful thing would make a tough woman like her cry in the corner of that ratty office. To talk to her without having to be rude for the sake of Rhett and Kirk. They would hurt her the second they suspected he harbored feelings for the curvy blond human bartender that he'd been watching from a distance for the last three years.

What could he possibly want?

Layla, holding a baby he put in her.

Life didn't work like that for a marked silverback, though.

****

In a daze, Layla stumbled back out to the bar and relieved Jake from making drinks by himself. People were pouring in, and the Beck Brothers were set to start performing any minute now. Nate, the cook, was running ragged with orders in the kitchen, and the minute Layla stepped behind the bar, she was bombarded with drink orders.

This was where she thrived. Good under pressure, she began pouring and serving and talking. Collecting money, opening tabs, giving change, next order. This was where she could let her mind go amid the clink of glasses and the *tink, tink* of ice, the pour of the beer spout and the murmur of the bar. When Denison's first note rang out loud and clear, Sammy's erupted in cheering and whistling. The Becks always drew a big crowd.

Kong and his crew were still at the table in the corner, and every once in a while, the couple at the end of the bar stopped making out long enough for her to see him. And sometimes, he was looking back, always with a troubled look to his dark eyes.

He'd hugged her. Okay, it had been borderline painful and he'd been too rough with her hair, but he was a big, muscular man who had seemed taken with the moment. Because of his aloofness, she'd thought he hated her all these years, but he'd gone and crushed her to his chest and apologized for what she was going through with Mac. And even if it had been startling and hurt a little, it had made her feel better just to have someone care for that one minute. She went through everything alone so she wouldn't burden others with the problems she faced, but for that instant, it had been such a relief to share her vulnerability with someone else. And not just with anyone, but with Kong.

She heaved a breath as she began to pour another beer from the tap. Kong felt even more important now, but he'd told her it was dangerous to approach him. What did that mean? Maybe whatever kind of shifter he was couldn't be with humans. Or maybe his animal was out of control. Some of the bears were like that, too. The Gray Backs had all been wild before they had settled down with mates. One of them, Easton, still looked feral. Maybe Kong was afraid of his animal hurting her, which made the most sense. That hug he'd given her had jostled her mushy human frame pretty good. It had been comforting, but rough.

When she looked at him again, he was watching her, eyes slightly lightened from a soft chocolate brown to an eerie green color as he talked to Rhett the Chauvinistic Poop Flake.

She was surprised when Denison looked at her and announced it would be the second to last song. The night was coming to a close, and it had flown by. Probably because she was lost in Kong-land. She put in Denison and Brighton's burger basket orders to the kitchen, and when they ended their last song, she began closing out the tabs of customers who'd just come in to watch the live music. There was an hour yet until last call, but half the bar cleared out in a matter of minutes after the Becks thanked the crowd for coming out and turned off the amps.

After the rush died down, drink orders came in slower, and Jake didn't have to help behind the bar anymore. She turned up the television again for Barney and cleaned the bar between closing out the rest of the tabs of the concert-goers saying goodnight to friends and trickling out of the bar. Kong and his crew were still here. She knew because she couldn't keep her attention away from him for long.

"Last call," she yelled over the sound of Kong's crew laughing over a game of pool in the corner. Her crush was sitting at the table near them, looking somber as he studied the label of his beer. Usually, he was happy and animated with the people around him. He seemed like one of those genuine nice guys who talked respectfully to the women in the shifter crews and was apparently good friends with some of the men. Or males? She wasn't really up on shifter lingo, though she supposed she should be. This was the biggest gathering of registered shifters in the world, right here, at the bar she worked, and she suddenly felt as if she knew almost nothing.

"Jake said to give this to you," Denison murmured, slapping three ten dollar bills onto the counter next to his half eaten burger basket. He shoved the rest of the money in his hand deep into his pocket. Jake paid the Becks better than the last boss.

"Thanks," she murmured, tucking the

money into her pocket. "Can I ask you something?"

"Shoot," Denison said around a bite of extra rare burger.

Brighton ate silently beside him.

"Do you call shifter girls women or females? And do you call them mates? And if you find your mate, do you marry them, too? Or is that just some human custom you find silly?"

"Whoa, woman, slow down. Why the sudden interest in shifters?"

Unable to help herself, she ghosted a glance to Kong, then made herself very busy wiping down the sink behind the bar to hide the heat in her cheeks. Thank God for dim lighting.

When she looked back up at Denison, he was chewing slowly, staring at Kong with a slight frown. "Layla, I consider you a friend."

"Me, too," Brighton whispered.

"We've known you for a long time, and you were awesome to us when we came out to the public. It didn't get by us that you were a big part of integrating us into Saratoga. You fought for us to keep playing our gigs, and you fought against the town vote to keep us out of the bar. So I'm going to give you a bit of advice." He inhaled deeply and leveled her a look as he leaned over the bar. "That one ain't for you or any other woman in this town. He's already claimed."

Her breath caught in her throat as something green curdled her stomach. "By who?"

"His people." Denison leaned back on his barstool and took another bite. "If it's a shifter you want, Layla, you'll have to go after a Boarlander."

"Denison, you know me better than that. I'm not a groupie." She lowered her voice to a whisper. "It's not his animal side I'm interested in."

Sadness pooled in Brighton's green eyes, and he lifted the corner of his mouth in a sympathetic smile. "It would be different if he was like us."

"Brighton," Denison warned.

The twins went back to finishing up their food, and Layla counted down her drawer in a daze. The bar was a ghost town by the time the Beck Brothers started packing their guitars into hard cases and coiling the sound system wires neatly to prepare for next week's show. They were much tidier than Jackson. Barney paid in cash, and just like every other night,

Layla called his brother to come pick him up so he wouldn't drive home sloshed. And when she turned from the phone on the wall, Kong was there, eyes lightened to a muddy green color and wariness etched into every facet of his face.

His lips were set in a grim line as he leaned against the bar top. "I need to close out our tab."

"Oh. Right." He wasn't there to share another unforgettable moment like earlier. This was business. She grabbed his credit card, charged it, and printed out a receipt.

He lifted a brief flicker of a gaze to her, then signed the receipt with a pen she'd slid toward him.

"So," she said nervously. "The show was good tonight." She kicked herself for her lame conversation skills. She could talk to anyone other than Kong—the one who mattered the most.

Kong gave her a warning glare, then slammed the pen down and turned for the door. "Let's go," he clipped out to his crew, who were watching them from beside the pool table.

"Have a good night," she called.

Rhett turned around right before he

walked out the exit behind the others and threw her a hate-filled glare. What had she ever done to him?

Baffled, she yanked the receipt off the counter and turned to the computer to enter in the tip.

$500.

Layla blinked slowly to ward off the hallucination, but nope, it was still there. In the *tip* field, Kong had definitely and clearly scribbled in *$500*, then added it to the twenty-seven dollar bar tab on the *total* line.

"Wait, what?" she murmured, lifting her frown to the door where Kong had disappeared. Why the hell would he give her such a ridiculous tip?

"Holy shit," Jake said from over her shoulder. He plucked the receipt from her limp grasp. "I think that's a new record."

"I'm so confused. He never even talks to me," she murmured.

"Maybe he just has money to burn," Jake said in a stunned tone.

"I can't accept this."

"You have to. He already left, and I can't keep it in our books. The paperwork won't match up. Damn, Layla, looks like you just had your biggest night."

"I'll say. Six hundred thirty-seven dollars in one shift thanks to that tip and the thirty bucks you gave me for making a fool of myself. That will pay more than half of Mac's mortgage." But she couldn't take it. She wasn't some charity case, and she hadn't earned this money. A tip, yeah. Five bucks. Maybe ten at the maximum if he was feeling generous. But five hundred dollars? That was insane and way too much. "Do you know where Kong lives?"

"Nobody knows where he lives. Even the bear crews are hard to find in Damon's mountains. And besides, you shouldn't be tracking him down to give him his money back. If he gave you this, it's for a reason. Let him do something nice."

"Jake, it's too much, and it doesn't feel right. I can't keep this."

Jake narrowed his eyes and sighed. "I forget what an Honest Annie you are. It's annoying."

"Jake, you know everything about the shifters. Where can I find him?"

Jake inhaled deeply and then let it out in a long, irritated breath. "You know that big barn off the old highway? The one near the gulch?"

"Yeah. What about it?"

"A man named Judge holds fight nights there on the weekends. Real backwoods shit, so it ain't safe for you to go alone. Kong usually fights last. Judge likes to pin him against any Boarlanders looking to make a quick buck. Kong is the fighter who draws the crowd and keeps them there betting. It'll take me a while to close up, but maybe we'll make it in time."

Layla couldn't wait on Jake to close up the bar, though, and risk missing her opportunity to give Kong his money back. She wouldn't be able to sleep tonight with that charity money taunting her. "Thanks, Jake," she rushed out as she pulled her tips from the drawer and yanked her apron off.

"Where are you going? I said it was too dangerous for you to go alone!" Jake called as she bolted for the door.

"I'll be fine!" She hoped.

THREE

Cheering echoed from the dilapidated barn through the field to where Layla parked her Civic at the end of a row of cars and trucks. The grass was tall but trampled down by tires as she made her way through one of the tread marks toward the old gray building. If it had been painted, the weather had stripped it away at some point in its history. There was a thin trail of people trickling inside in clusters of twos and threes, so she followed them around the side where two doors had been slid open, revealing a warm glowing light from inside. The building had probably housed eighteen horse stalls before Judge had turned it into a fighting ring. There were still a few stalls on the opposite side that were intact, but the rest had been torn out and tall metal poles held the barn upright now. The crowd was gathered around the middle, but she couldn't see anything from here.

The cheering and jeering was deafening, but she could make out the chanting from a group of spectators on the other side. "Kong, Kong, Kong."

With a gasp, she lurched forward and muscled her way through the mob. The closer to the ring she got, the harder it was to move anywhere.

"Hey!" someone behind her yelled. "Bartender!"

She jerked around to a familiar face. He was one of those frat boy types. Blond hair, blue eyes, cocky smile.

"Snakebite?" she asked, recalling the potent lager and cider drinks he'd ordered while he was watching the Beck Brothers.

"Yes! You remember."

She waved politely and turned to try to get closer to the ring. Only a couple of rows of too-tall men were blocking her from what sounded like a good fight if the cheering was anything to go by, but no good. She couldn't get any closer.

"Let me," Snakebite said too close to her ear as he gripped her waist.

She squeaked as he shoved her through a

tight hole between two behemoths. He yelled something at the pair of cheering tatted-up bikers as she wiggled past, but she couldn't make out what he said. As her focus pinpointed on Kong, the noise around her died away.

Shirt off, he was bleeding freely from a gash under his eye down his bare chest. A tattoo ran from his shoulder to his elbow, but she couldn't tell what it was from here. All black ink and tribal looking, it was just a blur of sexpot as he ducked a hit and swung hard enough to splinter his opponent's ribs. Kong's eyes glowed a brilliant green, and if she'd had any question before now about him being a shifter, the unsettling color that had replaced his soft brown eyes would've put those doubts to rest. His torso was thickly laden with muscle, his abs flexing with every graceful punch he threw and every breath he took. His waist tapered severely from the width of his shoulders, and she was stunned by how powerful he looked like this, slick with sweat, bloody, smiling, and egging on the titan he was boxing.

Harrison! She nearly swallowed her tongue as she realized Kong was fighting the alpha of the Boarlanders. Holy shit!

"Damn, Bartender, you're looking hot tonight," Snakebite yelled over the sound of the crowd.

Fantastic. She plucked his hand off her waist and tried to sidle away from him, but there was nowhere to go. It was too tight here, and she was getting pressed against the wooden railing as the men behind her surged forward and raised their fists in the air, chanting Kong's name.

He ducked and connected, volleyed and took a hit to the jaw that would've knocked her out cold. It hurt just watching. And now she was worried he would get hurt, or worse. Didn't people die from boxing? *No, settle down. Jake said he does this regularly.* He would be fine, and oh! Kong swung around and nearly ran into the wooden railing that was driving into her hip bones as the crowd pushed harder against her. A sickening noise sounded as Harrison went to town on Kong's stomach, blasting his fists against his abs.

"Come on," she murmured under her breath. Kong could do this. Sure, Harrison was a dominant alpha grizzly shifter, but Kong was…well…Kong. She'd never seen anyone stronger.

Kong jerked his gaze to her, and for an

instant, their eyes locked. She could see herself reflected in the churning green there, just before he grunted in pain and took a hard hit to his face.

She gritted her teeth and closed her eyes. They were so close, so violent, so powerful, and she was pinned here, unable to escape if she wanted to. And Snakebite was slithering his arm around her waist again.

Kong shoved Harrison and then thundered toward him, powerful legs flexing against his ripped, blood-splattered jeans.

She couldn't breathe. "Get off me," she rasped out, shoving Snakebite's hand off her ass.

"Don't be like that," he said in her ear, right before he drew her lobe between his teeth and sucked.

Layla yanked away, but the drunken idiot had bit down and pulled too hard on her stud earring. "Shit!" she gasped, holding her ear. When she pulled her hand away, a smear of crimson glistened on her index finger.

"A little pleasure, a little pain?" Snakebite slurred, wrapping his arms around her and pulling her hip hard against his erection.

"Are you fucking kidding me? Get off!"

"I'm trying to!"

With a screech, she slapped his face with her claws out.

"Bitch!"

She couldn't breathe, couldn't breathe.

When Snakebite grabbed her hair, she closed her eyes, waiting for the slap. Other than a stern yank to her tresses, the pain never came, and when she opened her eyes, Kong was throwing Snakebite into the horde of onlookers on the other side of the arena. Harrison was knocked out cold on the red saturated plywood floor with a few of his crew around him, and eek! Now Kong was headed her way with the furious look of a berserker in his eyes.

Retreat time.

She turned and ran forehead first into a solid wall of smelly biker.

"Kong!" Rhett roared from across the arena.

"Give me a fucking minute!" Kong yelled from way too close. Shit, shit, shit.

A meaty hand wrapped around her upper arm—all the way around it—and then Kong shoved her forward through a hole that magically appeared in front of her. Huh. This was much easier with a beefy, scary-ass, devil-eyed boxer giving death glares to anyone who stood in her way.

"Kong!" Rhett yelled again, from farther away this time, but when she turned to see how close Rhett was, Kong was blocking him from her view with his half naked body.

A squirrely man with greasy hair and a gap-toothed grin for Kong weaseled his way through the crowd. "Your cut," he said simply, slapping a wad of bills into Kong's hand. "See you next week."

"Yeah," Kong said in a low, rumbling voice.

He didn't even slow down as he collected his winnings, just shoved her forward faster. "Run," he demanded as soon as they were outside.

Run? "What's happening?"

"Fuck," he muttered when she apparently wasn't going fast enough. He wrapped his oversize hand around hers and yanked her forward until she was sprinting behind him. He shoved her into the passenger side of an old glossy black Camaro, slammed the door, bolted around the front, and then jammed the key into the ignition. The engine roared to life so loudly she put her hands over her ears.

"Buckle. Now." Kong's eyes looked terrifying as he glared at the back window behind him and blasted out of the make-shift parking space. The instant he hit the gas, the back two wheels spun out in the damp field, and the car fishtailed for a few seconds before he hit the worn treads and hauled ass out of the parking lot.

He checked the rearview mirror three times as he hit the main road, then slammed his open palm against the steering wheel. "What the fuck were you doing there?"

Layla was plastered against the door with her lips pursed. They had to be going eighty on an old back road with no street lights. Heart in her throat, she pulled the wad of cash from her pocket. "I came to give you your tip back."

Kong's eyebrows were dark squiggles of undeniable irritation when he glanced over at her. "Are you out of your mind? I told you never to approach me again. You didn't even wait three hours to come after me!"

She made an offended noise in her throat. "And what if I'd just been there for the fight? Wouldn't you feel super stupid right now for dragging me into your…your…" She looked around the perfectly detailed dash and fragrant black leather seats for inspiration. "Sexmobile!" No. Not the right word when she was angry.

"You were the one who brought that

gropey asshole—"

"I did not bring him. I served him drinks tonight, and he recognized me on the way in. I didn't invite him to grope me."

"Well, that's what happens there, Layla. It's not a place for a woman like you."

"Like me? You don't even know me. That might be just my scene."

She tried to hand him the money again, but he shoved her hand away.

"I'm not taking it back, so stop it." He jerked the wheel and took off down another back road, washed out and overgrown by brambles.

"Where are you taking me?"

"I don't know! Fuck, Layla. I tried to warn you. Did you not hear me when I said you have to stay away from me?"

"Yeah, but then you gave me five hundred dollars! I can't accept that. I'm no charity case."

Kong pulled behind a clump of trees and cut the lights. He stayed perfectly still, looking out the back window for a full minute before he slumped back against the seat. He slammed his head back against the rest and sighed. "I didn't give you the money to make you feel like a charity case. It just sounded like you could use the money when you were on the phone earlier. I have plenty, so I was just trying to help."

"You have plenty? Please don't tell me you are some trust fund prick who has a billion dollars stashed away in Swiss bank accounts."

"And if I was?" he asked, frowning so hard a wrinkle indented on his forehead.

"Then I'd be super prejudiced against you." A small smile cracked her face, so she crossed her arms over her chest and tried to keep the laugh securely in her throat.

"I own the sawmill. It's not trust fund money. I work my ass off and live below my means so that I can put extra away in savings, you judgy little thing." But the way he muttered the last part sounded like he was more amused than angry.

"Okay, then why are you fighting grizzly alphas for"—she yanked the wad of cash he'd shoved in the cup holder between them and counted it out—"a hundred dollars a pop?" She reared back. "A hundred dollars? Really? Your face looks like a murder scene," she said, gesturing at the gash in his eye, which looked half healed already but was still super gory.

"It's not about the money." He gripped the wheel, then let his hands slide off to rest on his thighs. "I have to fight."

Layla swallowed hard and leaned her cheek against the leather seat, pulling her knees up to her chest. "Why?"

Kong rolled his head toward her. "I just do."

"Because of what you are?"

"I'm human."

"Bullshit. Your eyes look like those bug lights that zap anything that gets too close."

His eye twitched as he ripped his gaze away and slid on a pair of sunglasses. "We shouldn't be doing this."

"You were the one who kidnapped me against my will."

"You smell like arousal and pheromones. Don't give me that kidnapped against your will shit."

Layla nearly choked on air. "Excuse me? I do not smell." She sniffed her arm but she smelled like she always did after work. Beer and deodorant.

"Quit sniffing yourself. I didn't say it was a bad thing. Just that we shouldn't be here, in this position."

"And what position is that? We're talking in a car, not banging on the hood." Though, now that she thought of it, that sounded kind of awesome.

"Stop talking," he muttered, turning the volume up on a country song. He gripped the wheel again and let off a slow breath.

"You're rude." Layla kicked open the door and marched off in the direction of the road. She wasn't just some shifter groupie he could treat like she was beneath him. He'd ignored her in the bar for years, and now he thought he could tell her to stop talking? No. She liked him, a lot, but she liked herself better.

"What are you doing?" Kong asked from right beside her.

"Hoooly shhhh—" she said, jumping and clutching her chest. It was dark out here, the moon only half full, and with her unimpressive night vision, she hadn't even seen him coming up on her right. "I'm going home."

"You're mad."

Layla rounded on him. "Damn straight I'm mad. I've tried to talk to you for years, and you've shut me down, and rudely at that. I don't know what your problem is, but you can't tell me to stop talking and just expect me to obey you, just like you can't tell me not to approach you and just expect me to heed your demands."

"I'm only going to get worse with age."

Layla waited for him to explain, but when

he didn't, she shrugged her shoulders and started walking again. "I'm out." She skidded to a stop and rounded on him again. "No, you know what? I thought about that stupid hug in Jake's office all night. I don't even know why. Fifty times at least, I've imagined you holding me, and then it happened, but you followed it directly with 'never talk to me again.'" Stupid tears burned her eyes, and she blinked hard to keep them where they belonged. "And it didn't even feel that good. You were too rough."

His eyes had dimmed to muddy green, and he arched an eyebrow. "You don't like rough."

"No. I like gentle. I'm not fragile, but I have to deal with a lot of shit in my life, and I want a man to be easy with me."

"Easy isn't in my nature and, again, I'm only going to get worse with age."

Layla stomped her boot. "What does that mean?"

"I'm a gorilla, Layla." He canted his head and searched her face. Moments of silence dragged on between them before he whispered. "I'm a gorilla shifter. And I'm not some blackback young buck either, woman. I'm a fully mature silverback. I'm physically and emotionally ready for a family group of my own with females who don't mind rough. I fight because I have to, because my animal requires it, so I can stay steady and in control, and so I keep fit enough to protect a group of females from other males or, God forbid, from humans who find out about us and want to hurt us."

"Females, plural?"

He dipped his chin once, his now dark eyes churning with sadness.

"King Kong," she murmured, feeling stupid for not catching it before now.

He nodded again.

"So there was never a chance for us to…"

He shook his head slow, lips pursed into a thin line.

"You can't be with humans anyway, can you?"

Kong scratched the back of his short, dark hair in agitation and stared off into the woods. "It's not like I chose this, Layla. I wish I was born a bear shifter where I would have more freedom to be with you, but who I breed with isn't my choice."

"Breed with?"

He nodded again, looking ill in the blue moonlight. "I'm ready for kids, but it's more than that. There is a leader of my people, a woman. She got to where she is because she's the cruelest of all of us. She's killed anyone who has opposed her. That woman is in charge of genetics and forming family groups. There aren't many of us, so if we're chosen for a duty, we have to do what she says. And when I was born, I bore the mark of the Kong. This stupid birthmark on my back that she determined means I'm the Kong. The Lowlander Silverback."

"Do you want to…breed…lots of women?"

"No!" Kong gripped the back of his head. "God, no, but that's the way it is for us. Shit." He slammed his shoulder blades back against the trunk of an ancient pine tree. His voice echoed with hollowness when he said, "I won't even be involved in my kids' lives like I want to. I'm there for two things. Fucking and protection. When Fiona calls me up, my life in Saratoga is over."

"But what about your sawmill? What about your friends here?"

"I'll have to sell and say goodbye."

"This isn't fair. It's not." Layla shook her head over and over in disbelief. Kong wasn't just unavailable. He was on-another-planet unavailable. But it wasn't just herself she was devastated for. Kong's life echoed with emptiness. How sad that he wouldn't fall in love or raise his kids. How sad that he would have to give up the life he'd built here for some archaic tradition.

How utterly sad that he didn't have any choice in his life.

Heartbroken, Layla murmured, "I think you should take me home." Because getting to know Kong better out in these dark, secret woods was only going to make it harder to say goodbye when he was called up to leave Saratoga.

He was quiet for a long time, leaned against that tree, staring at her with an unfathomable expression. He opened his mouth as if he wanted to say something, but closed it again and dropped his gaze to the ground. "Okay, Layla. I'll take you home."

He sauntered off toward his car, leaving her to trail behind. And that's when she saw it for the first time. The long, dark birthmark down his back that tapered into a smattering of constellation shapes just above his left hip.

The mark of the Kong.

Three years of adoring a man who wasn't only separated from her by species, but by tradition as well.

The mark of the Kong said he wasn't meant for her at all.

FOUR

The unfairness of it all socked Kong in the stomach and took his air. Layla was quiet and somber in the seat next to him as he drove her down the back roads toward Saratoga. As an apology, he wanted to hold her hand, gently even, if that's what she needed. If he'd been born different, he wouldn't be hurting her now. He could make her happy. Make her smile.

Every time he looked over at her, she was staring out the window with her arms clutched around her middle like she felt as gut-punched as he did right now. Her soft blond waves were covering most of her face, and his fingers itched to tuck the strand behind her ear and out of the way.

Something was wrong with him. Pairing up wasn't supposed to be emotional. It was supposed to be learning to balance several female personalities as they figured out how to be a family group under him. It was supposed to be getting them pregnant when they went into heat and making sure they were safe and provided for. It was supposed to be detached. Eat, fight, sleep, screw.

So why had he, of all the males, latched onto a lone human female? It didn't make any sense. Maybe it was because he'd been hanging around the bears too much. Watching each of them pair up with a mate they would go through life with, his heart had softened and changed. Now, he wanted a female to protect and love, too. He wanted one woman to bear him offspring. One woman who would let him hold his young and help raise them to be proper little gorillas.

He wanted Layla.

His mood darkened by the moment. His interest in the soft human beside him could get her killed, though, which in turn, would feel like it had killed him. God, he hoped he'd hidden her well enough on the way out of the barn. He hoped with everything he had that Rhett and Kirk hadn't seen Layla there at his fight.

"This is me," Layla said softly.

Kong leaned forward and studied the trio of beige bricked duplexes. The small complex was just outside of town, and behind the houses was tall pine wilderness. He cut the engine, and before she could escape, he said, "I was telling you to stop talking so I could focus. You were talking about banging on the hood of my car, and after fights, I'm already riled up. You're right, though. Doesn't matter the reason, I shouldn't talk to you like that."

Forcing his hand to be gentle, he tugged at her lobe and studied the cut near her earring. "I wanted to kill that asshole."

She lifted her startled gaze to Kong, and her lips parted slightly. "Thanks for defending me."

Always.

"Goodbye, Kong." Layla got out of the car and Kong followed.

"What are you doing?"

"Walking you to your door."

A baffled smile eased across her full lips. "Like at the end of a date?"

Kong laughed and ran his hand over his hair. "This is the closest I'll ever get to one again."

"Well," she drawled out, staring thoughtfully at the door with the letter C on it.

"Would you like to come in for a cup of coffee? Or hot tea? I don't really know what you can and can't drink," she murmured with a self-deprecating shake of her head.

She was so fucking cute all shy around him now. Oh, she could charm customers at the bar when she had her bartender face on, but she'd never acted like that with him. With him, she seemed to walk on uneven ground, and he liked that she was off-balance when she was talking to him. He felt the same around her.

"Uhh," he said, searching the street for Rhett or Kirk's cars. If they had seen him leave with Layla, they hadn't figured out where she lived yet. "I probably shouldn't."

"Right." She nodded as though she'd expected that exact answer, and he hated himself for hurting her feelings again.

"Fuck it," he murmured. "Hot tea sounds good."

Her delicate eyebrows, just a shade darker than her blond hair, arched in surprise. "Really?"

"One date is all we have." And he wasn't ready by any means to say goodnight—and goodbye—to her yet. What was the harm in one mug of tea with her?

While she unlocked her door, he waited

with his hands behind his back to fight the temptation to touch her.

"Don't judge," she said. "I didn't know I was going to have company or I would've cleaned up."

But when he stepped through the door, he had to check her face to see if she was being serious or not. The wood floors were swept and glossy under the pristine white couch. Colorful throw pillows were stacked neatly in place on the comfortable-looking cushions. There was a vase of fresh flowers on a coffee table that was made of planks of refurbished wood with iron accents. A small television was hung above the white brick fireplace, and on the small dining table off the kitchen was a matching vase of similar yellow flowers. Other than a stack of books piled off-kilter on the table, everything looked tidy.

"Woman, you would feel a lot better if you saw my cabin right now. My roommates are slobs."

"You have a cabin?"

He smiled at the genuine interest in her voice. "Yeah. I have a piece of land closer to Damon's mountains."

"Is Rhett one of your roommates?"

"Yeah, I live with Rhett and Kirk. Again, not

my choice. Fiona assigned them to me when she chose me for the Kong."

"Oh." Layla set her purse down by a stack of mail and padded into the kitchen.

With a deep frown, Kong brushed the top letter away to reveal a red *open immediately* label on the next envelope. It was a late bill.

"Do you have a preference in teas?" she asked, her back to him as she rummaged through a cupboard.

"Uh, no. I'm not picky." He thumbed away a few more, and all of them seemed to be overdue. "Layla?" he asked, holding up a stack of them. "What's going on?"

Turning, Layla gasped when she saw what he held. She sucked in air as if she was going to give him hell for going through her mail, but then in a huff, she turned back to a box of tea she'd removed from the cabinet. "That's none of your business."

Kong tossed the mail back into the stack and strode for the kitchen. He pulled the half-wrapped tea bag from her fingertips and pulled her to face him. "Are you in trouble?"

"No. Things are tight right now, but everything will be okay. I'm handling it."

"Handling what?"

She sighed heavily and yanked her wrists

from his grip. "I didn't ask you to come in so we could discuss my finances. I wanted to get away from all of it for one night. Can't you understand that?"

Kong huffed a short breath. He understood the need for an escape more than she would ever know.

Not wanting to see the disappointment swelling in her sad blue eyes anymore, he pulled her in close, careful to be gentle this time. She was soft against him. Soft tits against his hard torso, and his boner was raging between them, but who gave a shit? Not him. "Tell me."

Her rigid body relaxed by a fraction. "Mac was my neighbor growing up. He was the one I was talking to on the phone when you came into the office. So when I was sixteen... I swear to God, Kong, if you think I'm pathetic or pity me after I tell you this, I'll never forgive you."

"I won't think you're pathetic. I promise."

"And I don't talk about this shit with anyone, so no sharing it with your roommates or the bear crews or whoever it is you talk with. It's a small town, and it's taken me a long time to get to this point."

"Okay, I swear I won't tell anyone." He was also trying real hard not to feel flattered since she was about to tell him things she didn't share with anyone else.

"When I was sixteen, my parents left."

"Wait. They left? Like, they just were out on parenting you anymore?"

"Yeah. They went on vacation and didn't feel like coming back to Saratoga. It's fine. It's...fine." She sounded as if she was trying to convince herself. "So they asked the old man next door to be my guardian so I could finish out high school here, and Mac was the one who took me in. He was a parent to me when my real ones bailed."

"Geez," Kong said, shaking his head. He couldn't imagine ever doing that to his kid.

"Mac went into hospice care a few months ago, and I'm trying to keep his house for him. I tried to break the lease here so I can move into Mac's house and just pay one set of bills, but the landlord will charge me a ridiculous amount of money to leave the duplex early. And my contract is up in four months anyway, so if I can just float us until then, I can start digging us out of the hole when I move into the house. But right now with his care bills, his mortgage, my bills and rent, things are just a little tight. And sometimes I get scared I won't keep the collectors off my back long enough to keep Mac's house. He's really sick. If he found out I lost the house him and his wife bought together, he might stop fighting for his life." Slowly, she wrapped her arms around Kong's waist and snuggled her face against his chest, softening to him bit by bit. "And it actually feels really nice to tell someone that."

Kong's heart beat erratically against his sternum. Could she hear it? Could she feel the vibration of how much she affected him in this moment? It was plain and obvious that Layla was much more complex than just some bartender with an easy smile. She was one of those good-to-the-marrow, decent people. The type of person who would shoulder a huge amount of stress to reassure an old man that everything was going to be okay. She didn't know it, but she'd just rocked Kong to the core with the admission of her daily sacrifices.

"Then why were you fighting my tip so badly? I don't understand. You could use that money to take some of the pressure off."

Layla sniffled, and that little sound pierced his heart. She brushed her knuckles under her lashes quickly and slid out from his embrace. "Sit on down, and I'll get you cleaned up."

"What?"

"You're all cut up," she said with a shrug as

she avoided his gaze.

Cut up? He looked at his reflection on the glass insert cabinet near the fridge and cringed. Some faux-date he was. Harrison had popped him good right under the eye in the fight, and it had been a gusher. The cut was mostly healed now and hadn't bothered him at all, but half his face was covered in a dried stream of crimson.

All he wanted to do right now was take care of Layla. To ease her burden somehow. Money? He could make all of her problems go away, but that wasn't what she wanted or needed from a man. And now he was utterly confused on what he could do to make her feel better. The hug had made her shoulders relax, but then she'd pushed him away.

He leaned back on the counter, mystified by the woman's needs. With gorilla females, they needed protection, sex, and to be provided for. He could protect Layla and could certainly provide for her, but she didn't want that. She was independent, and a gaping piece of him admired her for that. She didn't need his help. He crossed his arms over his bare chest as she filled up a tea kettle with water and then disappeared down a short hallway.

Pushing off the counter, he studied the

pictures stuck to her refrigerator with colorful magnets and clips. Most were of her smiling with a gray-haired man with glasses who, from the look on his face, truly adored Layla. And along the top was a row of postcards. Most were from Florida. He plucked one out from under a zombie magnet and read the back.

Miss you bunches. Merry Christmas. Mom and Dad.

The writing was scribbled and messy, as if whoever had written it was in a hurry.

"Pretty lame, huh?" Layla asked.

Kong jumped and turned a startled gaze on her. "What is?"

"Keeping their letters where I have to see them all the time."

"Do you talk to them on the phone?"

Her lips turned up at one corner as she shook her head. "It's easiest if we don't talk."

Kong dragged his attention back to the postcard. The only correspondence between Layla's parents and her. It was postmarked three days before Christmas a few years ago. "Easiest for you or for them?"

"Your eyes are glowing."

"Well, this shit pisses me off."

"Why? It doesn't piss me off. I have Mac.

Now sit."

Kong snorted an offended sound as he replaced the postcard under the zombie magnet. "I'm a gorilla, Layla, not a Labrador." When she lifted her eyebrows and waited, he growled softly and sat in a creaking chair at the table, clearly not made for weight like his.

With a distracted smile on her lips, she filled a bowl with warm water and pulled up a chair in front of him. She wasn't close enough for his liking, so he pulled the backs of her knees until her chair scooted toward him and her legs settled right in the apex between his. There. Better. His animal quieted the beating of his chest and settled inside him. Fight nights always riled him, but Layla was proving to be a worthy balm. Damn, she was close to his throbbing dick. *Focus. You signed a contract.*

"Tell me about your crew," she murmured as she dabbed a moist washrag under his eye.

"My crew or my friends?"

"You dislike Rhett?"

"And Kirk. They're my handlers, nothing more."

"Okay, then tell me about your friends. Your real ones. I've seen you with the bear crews at Sammy's."

"Matt is the guy I go to when I need to get

something off my chest."

"Matt Barns of the Gray Backs?"

He nodded slightly as she wrung out the water in the bowl and began the gentle stroking of his face with the rag.

"I wish they were my crew." Kong swallowed hard, but the words were already out there in the air between them. He'd never said that out loud before.

Layla stopped cleaning and looked up at him with startled blue eyes. From this close, he could see green flecks in the middle. Beautiful. He felt drunk. As if she'd given him a truth serum. Siren. Enchantress.

"The Gray Backs are notoriously violent misfits who don't fit in with any crew. I know because I've served them since before they registered to the public. Those are some scary bears."

Kong shrugged his shoulder. She hadn't seen scary yet. Hadn't seen the monster inside of him.

"Can I tell you something?" Layla asked as she began rubbing the washcloth gently down his neck to the red splatters on his chest. "I like the Gray Backs. Even wild, they've always been nice to me. Easton almost killed a man for groping my ass a couple of months ago. Or

Beaston, I guess they call him."

Pride and relief surged through him that she hadn't judged his pathetic want to be a part of a ragtag misfit crew. They were a mixed bag of nuts—the crazy kind. Bears with scars in their middles that made them dangerous to the world but not to each other. A human, a raven, and a little baby dragon who didn't fit anyplace else, and for some reason, Kong couldn't think of a better batch of people to surround himself with. Layla's approval meant more than anything in the world. He grinned, unable to help himself, and dropped his gaze so she wouldn't see how pathetic he was for needing to please her.

Layla lifted his chin, and her gaze dipped to his lips. Canting her head, she whispered, "You always smile for the shifters, but you don't do it around me."

Inhaling deeply, he gripped her hand, plucked the rag from her palm, and pressed her touch against his cheek because, damn it all, it felt so fucking good to be this close to someone who was so real. "I couldn't, Layla. And I can't again after I leave tonight. Any attention I give you puts you in danger, and if anything ever happened to you, I couldn't live with myself."

"You can protect a harem of female gorillas, but you can't protect me?"

A deep ache sliced through his middle as he shook his head in weak admission. There were too many of his people, and they didn't care about human casualties. Not when it came to the continuation of their shifter species. They would see Layla as a threat to their precious breeding program and eliminate her.

A wave of devastation darkened her eyes for a moment before she replaced it with an empty smile. He hated that one. She gave it to assholes who wouldn't stop hitting on her at the bar. She gave it to Barney at the end of the night when he was slurring drunk and pestering her. Kong didn't want her to have vacant smiles for him. He wanted the genuine one back.

Before he could change his mind, he leaned forward and kissed her. *Too hard, too hard. Be gentle with her. She deserves gentle.* Kong slid his hand up her neck and gripped it softly as he angled his head and moved his lips against hers. She froze under his touch, but then softened as she leaned forward and stood. Kong gripped her waist as she straddled his hips and settled right over his erection. Her arms tightened around his neck, and a soft, happy-sounding moan whispered up her throat. Damn, this woman...she was everything. Filling his head, pushing out thoughts of danger. She didn't grind her hips against him or push the kiss to be more than it was. She just seemed to want to be close to him, up against his skin. His inner gorilla was alert and ready, senses perked but quiet, enjoying the moment and ready to kill anyone or anything who interrupted it. Kong slipped his tongue past her lips and tasted her. Damn, she was perfect. Her body was calling to his, drawing out his needs. *Be gentle.*

He plucked at her lips, then froze when she disconnected and curled up against his chest, arms tucked in and cheek against his neck. He sat there, arms suspended in the air. What was happening to him? He'd felt protective before, but she was hugging him so strangely, as though she trusted him. As if he wasn't terrifying.

And then she whispered, "I feel safe when I'm with you."

Fuck. She wasn't safe at all, and this had been a really bad idea. What harm could a cup of tea cause? The worst kind since his inner monster was now laying claim to his mate. No, no, no, this wasn't supposed to happen. Silverbacks didn't do a single mate. They did family groups.

He was panting now. *Don't hug her. Wrap your arms around her warm body, and you're done for.* "I have to go."

Layla eased back, a frown marring her beautiful face. Big blue eyes, questioning, petal pink lips, rosy cheeks that were deepening with color by the moment. "Did I do something wrong?"

"No," he gritted out, "I did." He gripped her shoulders and settled her on her feet, then strode for the door. This was it. This was the goodbye that was going to save her life and end his simultaneously. He'd been careless. Gotten too close and was losing control. Losing his head. He couldn't protect her and make the right decisions if he felt numb like this around her.

She was dangerous to them both.

He ran his hands roughly through his hair and turned at the door, feeling like every step away from her cut a slice into his guts, exposing his insides to air. "Layla, I'm sorry."

She crossed her arms over her chest like a shield, and he imagined her doing the same when her parents had left. When Mac went into hospice care. When everyone in her life had left her, and now he was just another letdown.

He ripped his gaze away from her broken eyes and forced himself out the front door. He closed it and pressed his shoulders against the cold wood until he could see straight because his gorilla was banging on his insides. *Go back to her*, he roared from his middle. *She's ours.*

But she wasn't.

Layla deserved a normal relationship that didn't put her in the crosshairs of his murderous people.

She deserved better than he could give her.

FIVE

Layla adjusted the heavy satchel that held the library books she'd just checked out and switched the bag of breakfast to her other hand to give her numbing fingers a rest. She couldn't believe she'd forgotten about her car. Her poor Civic was still sitting all alone in the overgrown parking lot of the fight barn. She was going to have to mooch a ride from Jake after work tonight to go pick it up, but until then, she was hoofing it. Good thing Saratoga was a small town, and a double good thing she had a badass pair of sneakers. She'd already walked three miles with nary a blister.

The bacon was definitely going to be cold, but Mac's favorite nurse, Sherri, would let Layla heat it up. She was always nice to Layla when she visited. The sun peeked out from behind the heavy, dark cloud cover, making her squint against the blinding light. She pulled her sunglasses from her hair and slipped them over her nose, then checked her watch and picked up the pace. If she timed it right, she'd get there an hour before it was time for Mac's pain killers, and he would be completely lucid for her visit.

The rumbling sound of engines filled the quiet morning, and she turned on the cracked asphalt to see a trio of muscle cars coming her way. The first was a red Chevelle, the second a deep green Mustang with black racing stripes, and the third was definitely Kong's classic black Camaro.

Ripping her gaze away from the parade of sexy cars roaring down the street, she took a quick left and speed-walked away from the noise. This would lengthen her walk to Tender Care, but it was worth it if she could avoid the ache in her chest watching Kong drive by her without a single glance her way.

Two of the cars loudly drove right by the alley, but the third sounded as though it had pulled off somewhere. Maybe at the gas station she'd just passed. No matter. She was impervious to him. Kissing her and then bolting—the brute. She got it—he was marked by his people and their barbaric traditions, but these were modern times. He was a big ass silverback gorilla as well as a grown man, and she couldn't believe he couldn't make up his own mind on who he wanted to hug. And kiss. And dammit, boink, because she wanted Kong bad. She always had, but it was even worse after she felt how tender he could be when he kissed her. And that fight! All sweaty and sexy and bloody like a big old testosterone-filled, sexed-up demigod come to earth to wreak havoc on her ovaries. A man who could fight like a titan and kiss her like that was dangerous to her heart. Especially since he obviously wasn't going to stick around. She'd had enough of people leaving.

An engine revved, echoing loudly off the brick walls surrounding the alley. Layla jumped as Kong's dark-tint car bounced slowly through the mud puddles toward her.

His window rolled down, and there was the man himself in a tight gray V-neck shirt with reflective aviators hiding those sexy eyes of his. "Get in. I'll give you a ride."

"I thought you weren't supposed to talk to me."

A muscle jumped as he clenched his jaw and looked in the rearview mirror. "It's now or never, woman. My detail will be circling back any minute."

Layla squeaked and high-kneed it around to the passenger side. When she shut the door behind her, Kong eased through the rest of the narrow alley and asked her, "Where to?"

"Tender Care. It's off Eckle."

He tossed her satchel a glance and asked, "What's that?"

Biting her lip to stifle the butterflies flapping around in her middle, Layla pulled out a thick book. "It's a romance set on a pirate ship between a captain and a woman his crew kidnapped. Mac likes stories with adventure, but with romance too. They remind him of his wife. She used to read these kinds of books all the time."

Kong took it from her hand and studied the cover with a faint and curious smile before he handed it back to her and turned left. "You're up early."

"I'm a morning person. I didn't used to be, but Mac always made mornings before school fun, and I kind of like starting my day early. Lots to do before my shift at the bar tonight."

"You're working tonight?"

"I have a feeling you know my schedule."

Kong smiled again, just a ghost of one, there and gone. He didn't respond, though, which was answer enough. He'd been watching her as she'd been watching him.

"Sooo, ditching the detail to rub elbows with the human riffraff, are we? You're so bad."

Kong chuckled and surprised her to her bones when he reached over and rested his oversize hand on her thigh. His knuckles were swollen and cut. From the fight last night? She was wearing jeans with holes in them, and he worked a frayed part just above her knee with his finger, brushing her skin and making her stomach turn molten. "I wanted to say I'm sorry for leaving like that last night."

"You freaked out."

"I didn't freak out."

She gave him a pointed look, and he caved. "I freaked out. Look, I signed this contract. It's why Rhett and Kirk are here. Their entire job is to follow me around and make sure I don't break the contract."

"What aren't you allowed to do?" she asked, hugging the crinkling bag of Mac's breakfast tighter to her stomach.

"Have sex. Really, I'm not allowed to do anything intimate with a women. They call it tainting the seed."

She inhaled deeply. "Wow."

"Yeah, pretty crazy."

"Why did you sign it?"

"Didn't have a choice. My mom knew what my birthmark meant the minute I was born, but she ran away from her family group. She was different. She felt things differently, wanted different things than the family group provided for her."

"Like what?"

"Like love. She wanted a single mate. The group let her go because they thought she was a bad gorilla who would infect the others with her weakness. She didn't want me to be the Kong. She wanted me to have a choice, so she raised me outside of our people. I went to school with humans as soon as I could control my shifts, and anytime she felt other gorillas got too close, we packed up and moved."

"How did they catch you?"

"The nurse who delivered me had given me up when my mom had taken me from her family group. She told Fiona about my birthmark, and they let my mom think she was hiding me well enough all those years. Fiona tracked me down as soon as I hit breeding age though. I was twenty-three when she sicced a couple of mature silverbacks on me and hurt me until I signed it."

"How long did it take?"

"Layla," he warned.

"I want to know it all, Kong."

"Three weeks. I was ready to die before I signed my life away like that, but they brought my mom in. They threatened her, and I was too weak by that point to put up enough of a fight to help her. I signed it to save her life."

"At the expense of your own," she murmured, feeling nauseous.

"At the expense of my own," he repeated in agreement.

"What happened to your mom?"

"Fiona put her back in the family group she ran from. She likes it okay, but she liked her freedom more." He took a right on Eckle and gave her a quick glance. "I told her about you."

"You did? When?"

"I've talked about you a few times over the past year. She gets it. I'm different like her. She wishes I could settle in Saratoga. She says she wishes she would've cut the mark off my back when I was a baby. It got too big as I grew older."

"Oh, Kong. I thought shifters had it all figured out. The bears get along so well with their crews, and they're nice and decent and honest people, but it's not like that for all of you, is it?"

"No, not all of us. The bears are lucky."

"If you refused to take over your family group, what would they do?"

"Kill me. After they force me to watch them kill you."

"Jesus," she whispered. "So there is no choice then. You have to go."

Kong parked in a space at the back of the Tender Care parking lot. His massive shoulders lifted in a sigh, and he gave her a sad smile. "At least I had last night with you, and I got a few minutes this morning. It's more than I thought I would ever get."

"Kong, did you like me before last night?"

"What?"

"Don't think, just blurt out the first answer you think of."

"Yes."

"How long?"

"Since the first time you served me a beer at Sammy's. Three years."

"Shit," she said through her tightening vocal cords. "Me, too. And I feel different about you than I have with other men. Like I *know* you. And still, I can't have anything meaningful with you. I hate this."

"I do, too," Kong said, pulling off his sunglasses and folding them onto the V shape in his T-shirt neck. His face was black and blue, but it didn't make any sense. It was the wrong eye from the cut Harrison had given him in the fight.

"Kong!" she exclaimed in shock, brushing her fingertip over the discolored skin of his cheek. "What happened?"

"Ditching my detail last night got me punished."

"Oh, my gosh." She couldn't even imagine the kind of violence that would cause bruising like this to stay on his face so long. "But you have shifter healing. Why isn't it getting better?"

Kong laughed and shook his head. "Woman, you should've seen me this morning. I look fucking awesome compared to when I got home."

"But I saw you fight last night. You're a beast in the ring. How could Rhett have done this?"

"It was Rhett and Kirk, and I let them."

"Why?" she yelled. "Why would you let them hurt you like this?"

"Layla, it's okay." He twitched away from her fingertips and slipped his sunglasses back on. "They had to send pictures to Fiona to prove I was punished enough."

"How does Fiona know? You were only gone, what? An hour, maybe two?"

"Because Rhett is a rat prick who calls her anytime I step out of line. It's his job." His smile had turned to a grimace now. "Speaking of, I'm supposed to be getting gas before I start work at the mill. They'll get suspicious if I'm gone for too long. Is your car still at the old barn?"

"Yeah. I'm going to get a ride out there tonight to pick it up."

"Don't bother. Hand me the keys, and I'll get it to you."

"But what if your guards find out?"

"Let me worry about them."

"Okay," she said on a breath as she dug around her satchel. She handed him the jingling key ring and pushed on the door handle, but turned back. "In case this is the last time I get to see you, can I…"

A slow, wicked smile spread across his lips. "Can you what?"

"Since you already technically broke your contract last night, I was wondering—"

Kong leaned forward and crashed his lips onto hers, halting her words. A helpless noise wrenched from her lips as she pulled him closer. This man was good and decent. He took care of his family and put others above himself. He'd stayed away from her for three years for her own protection, but now she was in this. Lost in the flood of longing to be in his arms, feeling safe like she had last night. She gave no fucks about that contract he'd been beaten and threatened into signing. And she definitely didn't care about tainting his seed. Kong was hers. Meant for her, fitting perfectly here up against her.

She brushed her tongue against his, and a soft rumble rattled up his chest, sending delicious shivers up her spine. This kiss wasn't the sweet first kiss they'd shared last night. This one was primal and full of need because she might never see him again. Might never talk to him again. Out there, in the real world, there was a cinder block wall in between them, but here, in the dark tint of his car, they were okay. She could touch him, smell him, love him, and no one would know. No one could hurt them here.

She ripped off his sunglasses and ran her hands under the thin fabric of his shirt just to feel the hard ridges of his abs again. His hands were getting rougher by the instant as he shoved his fingers up the back of her shirt and unsnapped her bra. She gasped as his warm hand slid up her stomach and cupped her breast hard.

Kong's touch gentled immediately, and he dragged his palm out from under her shirt. He stared at his hand with a baffled expression, as if he didn't know how they'd gotten this far. He exhaled a shaky breath, shook his head hard and murmured, "I think I'd better go."

Layla's blood was on fire and her breathing erratic. "Three strokes, Kong."

His blazing green eyes lifted to her. "What?"

"You could've had me in three strokes." She shoved open the door and fumbled with the shoulder strap of her satchel. "I want to burn that fucking contract, just so you know." She yanked the bag of Mac's breakfast out of the seat. "I finally found a man I want, who I feel safe with, and I can't even kiss him without feeling guilty, and over what? Because I'm tainting you for other women? It's not fair." Okay, her voice was a little shrill, and she was rushing her words, but dang it all, after all these years, she was finally with Kong, and it was like hot and cold water being dumped on her head over and over. "And furthermore," she growled, leaning into the car, "when I think about you with those other woman you are about to start serial fucking, I want to punch everything. You don't belong with them! They aren't your destiny, Kong. I am." She slammed the door and stomped off toward the back entrance of Tender Care without looking back. Oh, she wanted to, but she wouldn't. She was out of this game.

It wasn't until she got through the doors that she remembered her bra was a-danglin' so she bolted for a three-foot crevice between a vending machine and a wall to fix herself.

Utterly frustrated, she took a deep breath, counted to ten, and straightened her spine. Then she walked down the echoing, sterile hallway to meet the one person in her life who'd never let her down.

SIX

"Dammit," Kong muttered as he watched Layla disappear through the sliding glass doors of Tender Care. "What am I doing?"

Putting her at risk and still pissing her off, and why couldn't he just leave her alone? He'd seen her walking down the main drag of Saratoga and pulled into the gas station without a second thought in his head other than *I have to see her again*. And not just see her, but talk to her and touch her, because when he was close to Layla, he felt a little less lost.

He hit the gas and pulled out of the parking lot, then sped through town to the sawmill. Kirk and Rhett were waiting in the office the second he got in.

"What took so long?" Rhett asked, blue eyes icy as he crossed his arms over his chest.

"None of your fucking business." Because Kong wasn't a liar, and he sure as shit didn't feel the need to explain every second of his life to his handlers.

"You need another lesson in ditching us?"

"It was a gas station, Rhett. You could've turned around." Kong sat at the desk and flipped through today's orders. Good, the Gray Back Crew was scheduled to drop a load of lumber this morning. He could use some normal conversation with normal-ish shifters. Not this combative crap he had to keep up with Rhett all the time. Kirk wasn't so bad. He was quiet and occasionally sympathized with him. He still did his job and had been fine beating the shit out of him last night, but at least Kirk looked sick about it. Rhett had beaten him with a ruthless smile on his face.

Someday, Rhett would find he was pushing the wrong silverback too far, though. And when he did, his ass better be ready to run because Kong's inner monster didn't take too kindly to being forced into submission for some stupid pictures of gore for Fiona. It had broken something in him last night to take it. Something that Kong didn't think could be repaired. His animal was getting harder to control, and he couldn't blame him. He was dominant, a berserker, and he was being beaten while down on his knees, cowed in front of a couple of lesser silverbacks.

And all for spending time with his mate.

"Don't you have work to do?" he barked at Rhett, who was still standing there glaring at him.

Rhett's face morphed into something feral, and his nostrils twitched as he locked his arms against the edge of the desk. "Be careful with her, Kong."

Fury blasted through Kong's veins as he stood and slammed his fists onto the desk. A crack blasted through the center of the oak under his hands. A long, low, uncontrollable rumble rattled his chest. "No, Rhett. It's you who should tread lightly now."

A slow empty smile spread across Rhett's face. He pushed off the desk, chin up as he looked down at Kong. He turned and sauntered out of the office with a cocky gait.

"Kong," Kirk whispered, shaking his head. "Rhett was fishing, and you just told him his hunch was right." He ran his hands through his shoulder length hair and looked shaken. "Don't see her again, man. Please." Kirk left him alone in the office, the screen door banging loudly behind him.

Kong picked up a paperweight that held down a stack of receipts and chucked it against the wall hard enough to blast a hole through it. Doubling over, he grunted in pain as his inner gorilla pulsed against his insides. He wanted to kill Rhett. He wanted to rip his limbs from his body one by one for even mentioning Layla. Gritting his teeth against the pain of fighting the Change, he splayed his hands on the desk and dragged in a long, steadying breath. He thought of her clear sky-blue eyes. Her smile. The way her wavy hair fell forward in her face when she looked shy. The way her mouth formed his name. *Kong.* He could almost hear the soft sound of her voice. Little by little, his insides uncoiled and the rumble in his throat died to nothing.

Kong.

"Kong!" Rhett yelled from the loading area outside.

His eye twitched, and his lip lifted in an uncontrolled snarl. He had work to do, though. This sawmill didn't run on dreams and wishes. It ran on blood, sweat, and hard work. He shoved off the desk, grabbed his clipboard, and strode out into the sunlight. The sound of the saw was a constant here, and Kirk was just warming it up now. They had big orders to fill, and a whole heap of beetle-infested lumber to treat. This was one of the only sawmills that tackled the monumental task. It was hard to do, but their ability to treat the ruined lumber and make it viable had put Kong's sawmill on the map.

He strode past the big saw where Kirk was loading up logs to feed into it. Past the stacks of uneven junk pieces locals liked to purchase for refurbished wood pieces. Past the two-by-fours and the four-by-fours and the logs for cabins. This place was chaos at any given time, but he loved it. Here, he knew where everything was. Every piece of lumber. The numbers were constantly changing as he got in new loads from the lumberjacks up in Damon's mountains and shipped them out to buyers, but he was good at keeping track—both in the books and in his head.

His phone chirped, and he pulled it from his back pocket. He didn't recognize the number. Probably a buyer. "Hello?"

"I just got off the phone with Rhett," Fiona purred through the line.

Kong's boiling blood cooled to frigid in an instant, and he locked his legs, skidding to a stop on the dirt.

"I'm disappointed in you, Kong. You've

done well to stay away from females all this time, and you've lost it right at the end."

"The end?"

"It's time. Your females have synced up their cycles and will be in heat again in the next couple of weeks."

"I can't do this."

"You can, and you will, because it is your duty. You signed the contract—"

"You made me sign it—"

"You paid in blood for denying the gift I've given you! Have you forgotten that, Kong? You fought your destiny, and it almost killed you *and* your mother. Don't force my hand again. Your life in Saratoga is through. Make the proper arrangements. You have a week to get back to Oregon and take your place as the Lowlander Silverback. And Kong?"

"What?" he gritted out as his world spun on its axis.

"You will be punished for your time with her." The phone clicked and went silent.

The roaring in his ears was deafening. Not because of the punishment that was coming, but for the empty life he'd just been called upon to lead.

Rhett stood leaned against a table with the corners of his mouth turned up in a satisfied smile. Kong forced his gaze away from him to stifle the urge to yank his lungs out through his chest cavity.

The next three hours passed in a blur. His mind was taken with a roiling storm of emotions. Regret that he'd gone into that office and witnessed Layla's vulnerable moment. Loss that he would never touch her, talk to her, or comfort her again. Desperation to hurry up and accept his lot in life so this wouldn't hurt so badly. He wished he could rip himself away from Saratoga now instead of suffering through the next week. He had to try and sell the sawmill and his cabin, though, and he wanted to say goodbye to the crews who had been such a huge part of his life here.

Kong nodded a greeting as an eighteen wheeler pulled through the open gates toting a towering pile of stripped lumber. Beaston was driving with his mate, Aviana, riding shotgun. Despite his misery, Kong smiled. It was good to see them again.

"How was the Grand Canyon?" he asked as he tossed the last two-by-four into a pile ready to pick up.

"Good." Beaston canted his head as he approached, his bright green eyes trained on Kong's face. "Why do you look broken?"

"Easton," Aviana said softly, holding his hand. "You shouldn't say that about people."

"No, it's okay," Kong said, shaking his head. He led them to a shaded area under one of the giant saws. It was a half built roof with beams exposed. Just enough of a shelter to keep the elements at bay while they worked to shape the lumber.

Rhett tossed him a hate-filled glance as he and Kirk began unloading the logs from the back of the big rig, but Kong didn't care. He only had to deal with the asshole one more week. That was the only plus to uprooting his life here. He wouldn't need guards anymore when he was servicing the females like he was supposed to. He would be the right proper cowed silverback then. Beaston was right to call him broken.

"Can I ask a favor while you are in town?" Kong asked.

"Yes, anything," Aviana said.

Kong handed her Layla's keys and murmured, "There is a green Civic parked by the old fight barn near the gulch. Can you make sure it gets to the beige duplexes off of Rind?"

"Of course," she murmured, pocketing the jingly keychain.

He sat on a crude bench as Beaston sat beside him, Aviana on her mate's other side.

"What's wrong?" Beaston asked in a hard tone.

Kong puffed air out of his cheeks as he watched his guards unload the truck a log at a time. "I just got called back home. I'll be head of a family group come next week."

"Congratulations," Aviana said in a sweet voice, though confusion swam in her eyes. She twitched her black hair and blinked slow, and he smiled at how raven-like she was, even in her human skin.

"Not congratulations," Beaston said softly. "Condolences. What about Layla?"

Kong jerked his attention to the wild-eyed Gray Back. He'd never told anyone about Layla, but Beaston was calling him out? "What about Layla?"

"She's the love of your life. Even human. Even soft and full of tears, Layla's good. You watch her like she's yours, so she is." Beaston leaned back against the bench and draped his arm around his mate's shoulder, then frowned at the two men unloading lumber. "I don't want you to go."

"I don't want to go either," Kong admitted low, leaning forward to rest his elbows on his knees.

"I could kill them for you." And there it was, the crazy side of Beaston that Kong adored. He'd said the words nonchalantly, but his offer wasn't to be laughed off. Beaston would really give a go at offing them if Kong approved.

He clapped Beaston's leg and leaned back with a private smile. "You're a good friend, but I have to handle this one my own. It's my duty."

"Bullshit," Beaston scoffed. "Layla's your *duty*. Her happiness is your *duty*. Her safety is your *duty*." He jerked his chin toward Rhett and Kirk. "No pretending those animals have anything to do with duty." Beaston stood and spat in the dirt. "Your face looks like shit." He pulled Aviana up and led her toward the now empty truck. Halfway there, he stopped and tossed Kong a glare over his shoulder. "Don't go." Then he shook his head and walked away.

"Bye, Kong," Aviana said with a small wave. Her eyes swam with sadness that hit him right in the gut.

Easton made sure Aviana was safely tucked into her seat before he strode around the front of his truck. He lurched at Rhett and snapped his teeth so close to his face, Rhett had to jerk back or get bitten. Then Beaston climbed up behind the wheel and pulled away from the sawmill. And right as he passed Rhett, Beaston stuck his middle finger out the window and gave him a feral smile.

"Crazy," Rhett muttered as he watched the truck pull away with his hands hooked on his hips.

Crazy? No, Beaston got things other people failed to. He had seen right through Rhett's façade straight to his inner asshole in no time flat.

Kong scratched his lip with the back of his thumbnail as he watched Beaston and Aviana drive away. He'd grown attached to so much here.

He would never find a way to satisfy the hole this place was about to leave in his life.

****

Kong paced in front of the hospital room, clutching the quickly written apology in his fist. He couldn't see Layla again. Not now. Not after the call from Fiona, but it gutted him to think of leaving her without a goodbye. Even if it was just a note passed through Mac.

Kirk was waiting in the parking lot in case he tried to bolt, but at least his handler had been kind enough to let him come into Tender

Care alone. There was no risk of him screwing up here. Layla was working her shift at the bar now and no threat to his handlers' jobs. She may as well be a million miles away.

Huffing three quick breaths, Kong knocked softly on the door that a nice nurse named Sherri had said was Mac's.

"Come in," a cracking, aged voice said.

Kong pushed open the door slowly and smiled, his chin to his chest so the old man wouldn't feel threatened. It worked on his people, but he didn't talk to humans much, so hopefully this would work.

"I thought you would pace those halls forever before you grew the nuts to walk in here," the old man said, his wrinkles deepening with a smile. "Kong, I'm guessing?"

"Yes, sir," he murmured, approaching the bed to shake Mac's offered hand. It was cold and frail in Kong's grasp, and he reminded himself to be gentle, like with Layla.

"Mac," the man said, gesturing to a chair beside the bed.

Outside the large picture window, the sun had gone down and the evening was doused in shades of navy. Inside the room, it was sterile and white, and Kong's work boots squeaked with every step he took toward the chair, but the soft glow of lights over Mac's bed warmed up the room. That and all the pictures pinned to the wall behind his headboard. Kong studied the ones closest to him and smiled in surprise. They were all of Mac and Layla. Some of them, she didn't look older than sixteen.

"My wife and I never had kids," Mac said with a dreamy look at the photo Kong was staring at. "We tried, but it didn't happen for us before she got sick. And then Layla came along, and I got my shot at raising one after all. Funny how things work out sometimes."

Kong sat down in the chair and relaxed into it. "She told me about her parents leaving."

Mac's lips ticked as he shook his head in disgust. "They weren't fit in the first place. Layla fell to pieces when they left, but me? I was glad they were gone. At least Layla had a shot of a couple of normal years before she went out on her own. It was late in her life to give her stability, but she took to it. Most kids would've acted out, but not her. She was a Steady-Eddie. Responsible beyond what the kids at her school were, but she'd already been on her own a lot by then." Mac swung his intelligent gaze to Kong. "I'm so proud of that kid I don't know what to do with myself."

Kong grinned and nodded. "She sure loves you."

Mac nodded slowly, thoughtfully. "Do you know what she does every morning, first thing?"

Kong shook his head. He didn't know nearly enough about Layla.

"She drives out to the cemetery and waters my late wife's grave. Gloria has the greenest patch of grass and the cleanest headstone. I used to do it. Every day I visited my wife because I still feel very much married. But when my health went, Layla picked up where I couldn't. She brings me pictures every time she visits, and my Gloria has different flower arrangements in every one."

Kong's throat tightened as he fell for Layla even more. She was a good one. A genuinely decent person. Perhaps she was the best he'd ever met, and he was saying goodbye in a letter.

"Can I ask you something?" Kong said softly as he fingered the folded paper in his hands.

"Sure."

"Why didn't you ever re-marry? Lots of people find someone else after they lose a mate, but you didn't. Why not?"

"Because my Gloria was it for me, son. And may you be lucky enough to find a woman like that. I had thirty good years with the love of my life. I lived an entire lifetime with her. Some men only get one big love, Kong. One shot at that kind of happiness. Anyone else would've just felt like filler until I died and joined Gloria again."

Mac watched him for a long time, but Kong couldn't speak. Not now when he felt like Layla was that for him. The other females were the filler, and he was choosing them over something real with her.

"Layla has talked about you over the years," Mac said quietly. "People don't affect her like they do you or me. She shut down after her parents left and became protective of her heart. But with you, I saw that spark in her eyes again. It was nice to see her open up about someone other than me. I was hoping she wouldn't be alone in this world when I go. This morning she said you would leave soon, though."

Kong nodded his head, a deep ache unfurling in his chest. "I've been called away. I'll be gone in a week." He made a single clicking sound behind his teeth and met Mac's sympathetic gaze. "I'm letting her down."

Mac's eyes rimmed with moisture as he pointed with a shaking, knobbed finger to the pirate romance Layla had gotten him from the library. "Read to me a while?"

Kong nodded and replaced the thick book on the end table with the goodbye note he'd brought for Layla.

"The second to last page of chapter sixteen," Mac instructed.

Kong flipped through to the right page and read aloud. "As he watched his love float away at the helm of the small tug boat, he knew he'd made a grave mistake. A necessary one for her since she would be better off safe on land than on the arm of a high seas criminal, but a detrimental one to him. With every stroke his first mate rowed her away from him, his heart turned blacker, darker, and more hollow as a pain reared up inside of him and became too harsh to bear. He was killing himself by sending her away but saving her in the process, and all because of who he'd turned out to be. So many decisions in his life that had gotten him to this exact moment in time would haunt him, but he couldn't regret the journey. The jagged road he'd taken in his life had led him to a few glorious moments with her. He'd lived more in the last two weeks than he had in the entirety of his forgettable life because he'd known love—the bone-deep kind that changed a man from the inside out. And now...he knew sacrifice." Kong's voice cracked on that last word, and he shut the book, unable to read anymore. He swallowed several times before he braved a glance back to Mac. "I'm sorry," he whispered.

"I'll give her the note," Mac said in a frail voice.

"Thanks." Kong stood and strode for the door.

"Kong?" Mac asked.

Kong stopped and turned, leaned on the door frame. "Yes, sir?"

"You should read the ending to that book someday."

Kong nodded, knowing he never would. "I'll see you when I see you, Mac."

The old man's thin smile lifted and fell. "Goodbye, Kong."

SEVEN

Layla was supposed to be off tonight, so when she bustled through the door and behind the bar top, Kong was utterly gut-punched.

"She isn't supposed to be working tonight," Kong muttered to Creed, dark-eyed alpha of the Gray Backs. "That's the only reason I was okay with having this here."

Jason was talking to Kirk in the corner while Kong shot pool with Creed. Beaston, the clever monster, had apparently told his crew about Kong's troubles, as well as about Layla, and they had set up a going-away shindig at Sammy's. They were also doing a bang-up job of keeping Kirk at a distance, which he appreciated more than they knew. Rhett had said he'd rather cut off one of his own balls than come to a Kong celebration, so he was getting a night off from that relentless prick as well. The going-away party had gone great until Layla came in looking like a million fucking bucks in a short, ripped-up jean skirt, fishnet stockings, and black combat boots that came mid-calf. And always with the tank top that showed the top half of those buxom tits of hers. And now, after one second of drinking her in, his dick was knocking on the seam of his jeans.

He forced his eyes back to the pool table to line up a shot before Kirk noticed his flighty attention. Willa danced by with a red feather boa around her neck singing a song about a matchmaker finding a find and catching a catch. He'd bet his sawmill the pint-sized red-headed hellion had something to do with Layla taking over Jackson's shift midway through the night. Kong hid a smile and shook his head as he popped the cue ball into the red three. It blasted into the corner pocket. Damn, he was going to miss these bears.

"We got you a going-away card," Willa said with a graceful spin before she leaned onto the pool table. She pulled an envelope from her bra and grinned up at him. "It's not money."

Kong snorted and ripped into the thick envelope. Inside the card read, *Don't Go*

Asshole in ugly bubble letters, and the Gray Backs and Ashe Crew had all signed it. In the very bottom corner, Beaston had simply written, *you are my friend*, and he and Aviana had signed their names underneath.

Kong's throat tightened, and he tried to smile at Willa. He opened his mouth to pop off a witty retort, but none came.

"Oh, hairy monkey," Willa murmured, throwing her tiny arms around his middle and squeezing him with an amazing amount of gusto for one so small. "This place isn't going to be the same without you."

"Willa, you're killing me."

She whispered, "It's okay to cry."

"No, I mean you're squeezing the shit out of me."

"Oh. Bear muscles," she explained, easing away and flexing. "As almost alpha, I don't know my own strength."

Creed sighed behind her and chalked up his pool cue. "Willa, you are *second*, not *almost alpha*."

It's all the same, Willa mouthed to Kong. She whipped her cell phone from her back pocket and nearly blinded him with the bejeweled case that protected it. She punched in a number and waited, hip cocked against the pool table as she bit her thumbnail. "Oh! It's ringing."

The landline behind the bar was trilling at the same time Willa shoved the phone into his palm and whispered, "Good luck."

"What?" he barked out as panic dumped adrenaline into his veins. But Willa was already prancing off toward Kirk, flailing her feather boa gracefully.

"Sammy's," Layla clipped out.

"Uuuuh, hi." He turned and shot her a glance behind the bar.

"I'm busy. Someone is apparently having a going-away party I wasn't invited to." Her voice shook with anger and something else he didn't understand. "Nothing like serving drinks at a farewell party for the man I love."

She made to slam the phone back onto the cradle nailed to the wall, but Kong said, "Wait." He rubbed his hand across his forehead and checked that Kirk was busy. Willa had draped herself across him, and Jason was singing in an off-key opera voice. Matt was in the process of positioning himself in between Kirk and Kong, cutting off his guard's line of site. Well played, Gray Backs. Kong turned and rolled his shoulders as he looked at the wall and lowered his voice. "I'm sorry."

"Yeah, you said that in the note. I got it by the way. Nicely done giving it to Mac instead of telling me in person."

"Because I can't," Kong murmured. "I can't see you. I can't talk to you. You think I want it like this? I fucking love you, Layla. I *love* you. I do. There it is." He gritted his teeth and murmured, "I've never said that to anyone before, and look at where it's getting me. I'm gutting us both."

When he ghosted a glance at the bar, Layla had her back to everyone, and her shoulders sagged. "How did everything get so fucked up?"

That would be his fault. Or rather the animal inside of him. The birthmark. The traditions of his people. All of it was on him. Layla was perfect. A perfect rose in a summer garden, and he was the weed steeling her water, her life, clinging to her roots until she suffocated.

"Do you know how hard it is to love a man I can't touch?" she whispered brokenly.

A soft growl rattled his throat, and he tossed a look to Kirk who was laughing with the Gray backs as Georgia sauntered over with a round of shots. She shoved two in Kirks fists as the rest of the crew lifted their tiny glasses and toasted him. It was now or never if he wanted to steel a moment with her. Rhett was back at the cabin, and Kirk was more relaxed in his guard duties, and if his slurring words were anything to go by, well on his way to three sheets to the wind.

"Meet me in the office," he murmured.

"When?"

"Now." He hung up the glittering phone and set it on the green felt of the table.

Willa gave him a wink when he muttered he was going to take a piss. Kirk didn't even respond, so Kong weaved through the crowd and into the back hallway. Layla was already waiting, pacing when he stepped into the office.

"The door doesn't shut," she whispered, her bright blue eyes round. She smelled like worry and adrenaline.

But Kong was a problem solver, and a forceful shove to the door sealed that sucker tighter than a tomb. As he turned, Layla slammed into his chest and wrapped her arms around his waist. Layla, his Layla. Damn this felt good, right here with her body wrapped around his.

"Why are you going now? I thought you would have more time."

"Fiona called me the day I dropped you off at Mac's. Rhett got suspicious I met someone and ratted me out. I think it sped up the process."

"I don't want them to have you. I don't want you protecting them. I want you for me," she said in a voice as soft as a breath.

Kong winced as his chest crumpled inward with pain. Damn, he wished things were different. He wanted her to be safe with him, but he was only one silverback, and Fiona could sic the entirety of his people on him, and on Layla, if he wasn't careful.

"I want you," she said, stepping back.

He angled his head and frowned. "What?"

"If this is all I have with you for our whole life, I want you."

"Layla..." Kong shook his head. "I signed..."

"I don't give a good goddamn about some contract you were forced to sign, and I give even less fucks about *tainting your seed*. You're mine, Kong, and if all you're leaving me with is a memory to last my whole life, I want a good one." She ran her hands underneath his shirt, over the ridges of his ab muscles.

His eyes rolled closed because, holy hell, she felt good against his skin. On her tiptoes, she kissed his tripping pulse at the base of his throat. His hands tightened around her waist. *Be gentle. Layla likes gentle.*

He'd prided himself on being an honorable man and following the contract, but it had all been shot to hell the day he'd given in and talked to his mate. He'd never wanted anything more than to bury himself deep in Layla and empty himself inside her, just to be close. Just to share a moment like that with the woman he loved before he ripped himself away from here and lived the rest of his life in numbing emptiness. Dammit, he wanted to feel! He wanted to know how mating should be. Not just some scientific humping to create offspring.

"Take off those fishnets, Layla," he growled out in a voice he barely recognized. Her scent was filling his head, making it hard to think.

Layla's pupils contracted. She swayed slightly, but regained her balance and began to kick out of her boots. Too slow.

With a snarl, he gripped the edge of the desk and shoved it against the door, then ran his hand over the surface, scattering everything onto the floor. He gripped her hips and slid her onto the table, then reached between her legs. *Riiip.* The fishnets weren't an obstacle anymore.

Layla gasped and slid her arms around his shoulders just as his lips collided with hers. These weren't sweet kisses like their first one had been. There wasn't time for that. He unzipped his jeans and pulled them down just enough to unsheathe himself, then he pushed her panties to the side—lacy if his sense of touch was spot on—and cupped her sex. He wasn't small, and he needed to make sure she could take him.

He pushed his finger into her. So wet. Warm. Fuck, he was losing his mind. He pulled out and slid two fingers in. Her hands were on his dick now, stroking as his lips moved against hers. He shoved his tongue past her lips as he jerked her to the edge of the desk. So wet. Wet and ready. The growl was constant in his chest, but he was in it now. If it scared her, she'd have to deal. This was him. This was what it was like to be with a silverback shifter.

He pressed the head of his cock against her, dipped inside by an inch. So tight. Fuck, she felt good around him. His hips jerked as he pushed inside her again. *Steady. Don't hurt her.* Layla arched back as his kisses trailed to her neck. He sucked hard as he pushed into her completely. That would leave a mark, but so fucking what? This was what he got with her, and he wanted a mark on her. He wanted her to look in the mirror and remember the exact second he took her. Claimed her. Claimed her? Yeah, that sounded right. She was his, and no one else for the rest of his miserable life would replace his Layla.

He grunted as he eased out of her. Wrapping his arm around her back, he pulled her closer and slammed into her. She was mewling, begging, but she had to be quiet here. He kissed her hard, bit her lip to remind her to be quiet. Shit, he didn't want that. He wanted her screaming out his name. He wanted her loud. His stomach flexed as he pushed into her again. Another sexy groan from Layla, and he was gone. Not thinking straight. Rutting like an animal, he pumped into her, careful to hit her clit every time they connected because, dammit, if this is all he could give her, she was going to come. He was going to take care of her. Satisfy her, satiate her— his animal required it. Duty. His duty shouldn't be to female strangers whose genetics made them a viable match. His duty was to his mate—the woman who had his heart. The only woman he wanted to breed with. His teeth were elongating, just the canines. He could feel the burning ache of them.

He wanted to bite her. It wouldn't Turn her. It would only show other silverbacks she was claimed. He wanted to mark her, but wouldn't hurt her, not when he couldn't stick around to defend his claim. He pumped into her faster, and she met him blow for blow, soft noises of abandon in her throat. *Don't Change. Don't scare her. Make her come.*

The growl in his throat was louder now, uncontrollable as pressure filled his dick. He was close, so close. He shoved her backward and laid her back against the desk. Jeans still clinging, he rolled his hips into her, locked his arms on either side of her head and watched her face as he took her. Bowed against the desk, she raked her claws against his back and exposed her neck. *Good mate. Just like that.*

His eyes would be blazing, and his teeth were long now. He should scare her, but when she opened her eyes to dazed slits, a wicked smile came over her face. "Do it," she gasped out.

Kong slammed into her again as punishment for asking for things she knew nothing about.

"I'm going to come soon," she said on a breath. "Do it."

Kong lowered to her, bucking into her. So wet, fucking her had a sound. Sexy. He teased, grazing his teeth against her shoulder. He gripped her hair at her nape, steadying her as he thrust into her hard enough to shove her up the desk toward the door.

"You don't know what you're asking," he gritted out. A few more strokes, and he was going to blow. So tight. So good. "It won't Turn you or fix things for us. It's not like that for gorillas. It'll only hurt and scar you."

Layla kissed his shoulder, then sank her teeth deep into his skin. Harder. He gritted his teeth at the pain. Harder still, she clamped down until the scent of iron filled the air. Little hellion human mate. What was she doing? Marking him so that every female he ever bred would see proof of his betrayal.

Good mate. Smart mate.

Holding back a roar, he sank his canines into her shoulder—shallow to keep her pain minimal, but deep enough that his teeth would leave four pink puncture mark scars. She cried out his name and clawed his back as her body clenched around his in deep, quick pulses. Her orgasm triggered his. He released her skin from his bite and pressed his forehead against hers, closing his eyes against the ecstasy as his dick contracted and shot jets of seed into her. Over and over, he pulsed into her, filling her until her legs were slick with him. "Fuck," he whispered, shaking as he bucked into her again, slower this time. He lifted off her by inches as he continued to stroke into her wet heat, uninterested in breaking their coupling yet. In and out, slower and slower until her aftershocks morphed into another orgasm. This one drew a gasp from her lips and his name whispered like a prayer. His Layla.

He sighed and rolled his eyes closed at the feeling of her clamping around his shaft, then opened them again just to drink in the soft glow of her skin. He'd covered her, broken the contract and bred her. And fuck it all, he couldn't find it in himself to feel guilty. Not now. This was the most real moment of his entire life right here, and he was bleeding onto her in a steady pit pat that slowly filled the hollow at the base of her throat. He inhaled deeply. "We're a mess."

And now it would be even harder to leave her.

Now, he didn't even know if he could.

EIGHT

How careless could she be? Kong had been warning her about the danger they'd be in if they got caught, and what did she do? Begged shamelessly for him to mark her.

A whimper clawed its way up the back of her throat as she pulled another wad of paper towels from the dispenser in the bathroom. Kong hadn't been lying about them being a mess. Her shoulders and chest were smeared with a mixture of hers and Kong's blood, and it had taken her a good while to shimmy out of her torn up fishnets and clean up her legs.

Her sex pulsed at the memory of him between her thighs, and she stifled a smile. That had been incredible. He'd been sexy and barely in control, stroking into her like he couldn't stop. For as long as she lived, she would never look at that office the same way.

Jake was going to kill her for breaking the grizzly bear snow globe she'd gotten him as a gag gift over Christmas, but she would replace it. Maybe with a gorilla snow globe.

"Come on," she muttered as the wad of paper towels refused to absorb any of the sticky crimson around the thin straps of her Sammy's work tank top.

A soft knock sounded at the door. That would be Jake wondering where the crap she'd gone off to when they were so busy. "Just a second!"

"Layla? It's me, Georgia. Can I come in?" Georgia was Jason's mate and one of the newest members of the Gray Backs. She was also a newly Turned bear, and Layla didn't know if Georgia could handle the scent of blood that even her dulled human senses were picking up.

"Uhh." Layla stared at her blanched reflection in the bathroom mirror. She hadn't managed to get the puncture holes of her bite mark to stop bleeding yet, and now she'd painted her skin with gore. "I'll be a few more minutes."

Georgia lowered her voice. "Kong sent me."

Layla flew to the door and pulled it open

by inches. Georgia stood there all wild curly hair, freckles standing out, and a sympathetic grin on her full, glossed lips as she held up a serious looking first-aid kit.

"Oh, thank God," Layla said on a relieved breath.

Georgia slid into the bathroom and locked the deadbolt behind her. "Jake is handling the front fine. Willa told him and half the damned bar you got your period. Barney looked nauseous. Take off your shirt."

"But I have to wear it. It's part of the uniform."

"You smell like fresh meat and Kong," Georgia said, popping the top to the first-aid kit on the counter. "Kirk is drunk as a skunk, but he'll smell you the second you go back in there."

Layla did as she was told and peeled her shirt over her head. "What about Kong? He's bleeding, too. Oh my God, Georgia, I lost my mind and bit him." In a horrified voice, she repeated the last embarrassing part. "Bit. Him. Like an animal."

A grin transformed Georgia's face as she pulled open a pack of cloths and began cleaning Layla's skin. "You want to know a secret?"

Layla nodded, feeling sick at the memory of how Kong's blood had tasted trickling into her mouth.

"I bit Jason, too."

"You did?"

Georgia nodded and wet the rags, then began scrubbing her again. "He had another mate before me. One who died, but she was horrible to him. I hated her mark on him, so I made my own. I was human at the time."

Layla snorted. "Georgia, what is wrong with us?"

"Not a damn thing. Your instincts kick up when you fall in love with a shifter, Layla. And Kong is fine. He's strutting around like a proud rooster, actually. He's already cleaned up and mostly healed, and his shirt is covering your mark. He's just worried about you."

Layla's sigh released a hundred pounds of weight off her shoulders. "He's proud?"

"Hell yeah, girl. He just bought the entire bar a round of drinks. And it's not just as a distraction either. I haven't seen Kong smile this much in months. I knew something had been eating away at him, but I didn't know it was you."

"Me?"

"Yeah, you. Now all his words of wisdom

for everyone make sense. He was in love with you and couldn't take his own advice because of his people. All he could do was make sure his friends didn't waste opportunities to be with the people they cared about. Hold this," she ordered, pressing a wad of gauze over the four puncture marks near the base of her neck.

Layla held it down hard as Georgia began scrubbing the blood from Layla's shirt under the sink water. When she was done, Georgia pulled her own black cotton shirt off and handed it to Layla. "Put that on. Jason's already waiting out back to take me home. I'm stealing your shirt for now."

"Thanks for doing this." Layla looked under the gauze with a wince. It wasn't bleeding much anymore, but it hurt like the dickens.

Georgia replaced the old with new bandages, taped it down, then helped her into the new shirt. "Don't favor it. Just do your best to make it look like you aren't hurting, okay? The Gray Backs will work on keeping Kirk schnockered." Georgia tossed all of the used medical supplies into the trashcan and buttoned up the first-aid kit. Then she turned and hugged Layla more gently than she would've expected from a grizzly shifter.

"Congratulations."

Layla hugged her shoulders as her heart sank down to her toes. "He still won't stay."

"But for tonight," Georgia whispered, holding her back at arm's length, "you belong to each other. Enjoy it and let tomorrow bring what it will."

Layla tried to smile but her lip trembled, so she nodded instead, fighting burning tears as the fear of losing Kong after what they'd just done seeped into her bones.

Head up and spine straightened, Layla followed the curvy park ranger into the hallway and waved her thanks as Georgia made her way to the back exit.

When she came out to the bar, Jake was in the middle of pouring a row of at least a dozen shots. He passed them out to the customers at the bar top then turned a wary grimace on her. "Are your female problems all…cleared up?"

Layla pursed her lips to contain her smile and nodded. "Mmm hmmm."

"Good. Now take this tray of drinks over to the pool table before they get warm. And what happened to your tank top?" he asked as she walked away, tray in hand.

She ignored him because, really, she was crap at lying. She licked her lips and smiled shyly as she set the tray on the table close to the group playing pool. Kong bent over to line up a shot but his churning green eyes lifted to hers, and in an instant, the worry there morphed into a heart-stopping smile. Her heart beat against her breastbone as she handed out drinks, and now her grin was uncontrollable. She'd been with Kong now. She'd shared one of those life-altering moments with the man she hadn't been able to stop thinking about for three years. He'd broken his contract for her and marked her. The bite on her shoulder burned and tingled just thinking about it, but she'd heard Georgia and pretended it didn't bother her at all. Later, she would be a total wiener and take pain killers, but in front of Kirk, she would be tough for both Kong's sake and her own.

"You," Kirk slurred, pointing unsteadily at her around Creed. "You're the reason for all the trouble."

The blood drained from her face, leaving her skin clammy and cold. "W-what?"

On the other side of the pool table, Kong stood to his full height.

"You…" Kirk closed his eyes and seemed to drift to sleep before he blinked them open again and took another pull of what looked like straight whiskey. "You're the reason I'm going to be punished. You're the reason you're being punished."

"What are you talking about?" Kong asked in a low, dangerous voice.

"Layla!" Jake called over the bar.

She ripped her gaze away from Kirk's bleary eyes and called, "I'll be there in a minute!"

"No, now. You have a phone call."

A phone call? It was midnight. The way Kirk shook his head and stared at her with that sad look in his eyes made her blood curdle in her veins. Chills blasted up her arms as she backed away with the empty tray. She turned and ran for the bar, then picked up the phone off the counter.

"Hello?"

"Layla," Sherri said, her voice shaking. "I tried to call your cell phone but you weren't picking up."

"What's wrong?"

"Honey." Sherri swallowed audibly. "Honey," she repeated softer, "Mac passed tonight."

Layla shook her head slowly back and forth. "No." The noise of the bar died to nothing as Sherri explained that he'd taken out his breathing tube. "No."

"He had a real bad day, and the pain killers weren't doing it. This afternoon he was having such a hard time breathing. I left you voicemails."

"No, Sherri," Layla said, wrapping her arm around her middle and doubling over. "I just saw him this morning."

"Baby, I'm sorry." Sherri was crying now. Layla could hear it in Sherri's voice, in the hitched way she was breathing.

"I'll be…" Layla squeezed her eyes closed against the pain in her middle. "I'll be there in a few minutes, okay? Just keep him awake."

"He's gone, honey."

"Keep him awake," Layla demanded as the room spun round and round. "I'll be there soon. It'll be okay. You'll see."

"Layla, I don't think you should drive—"

She hung up the phone in a rush and stared at the faded brown plastic of the landline. She was still shaking her head, so she stopped. Jake was staring. Barney, too.

"Are you okay?" Jake asked low, gripping her elbows.

Spinning room, spinning Jake. She wanted off this ride.

"Yeah," she said in a hollow tone she didn't

recognize. Was she speaking, or had she only imagined her words? "I'm fine." Head bobbing. *Harder. Nod, and he'll believe you.* "I have to go. I'll be back soon."

"Okay," he said, eyes wide. His gaze drifted to the phone and back to Layla, but she was already backing away.

She turned and bolted for the hallway. Someone had tidied up the office where her purse was sitting in the bottom drawer of the desk. Kong? Georgia? She snatched the purse and sprinted through the bar as the first wave of tears burned her eyes.

Mac wasn't dead.

He couldn't be.

This was all just a misunderstanding.

NINE

Kong followed Layla's exit with his gaze until she was gone out the front door. A feeling of wrongness filled his instincts, and he leveled Kirk with a suspicious glare. "Where's Rhett?"

"He didn't want to celebrate tonight, Kong. He never wanted to be here, remember?" Kirks words tumbled over each other, one word slurring to the next. "He had orders. Fiona told you. She told you."

Kong ripped him out of his seat, clenching his shirt as he brought him face to face. "On pain of fucking death, you better tell me where the fuck Rhett is. Now."

"I told you. Carrying out orders."

Kong threw him back into the chair and scrubbed his hand over his two day scruff, pacing tightly as he stared at Kirk.

Kirk looked sick when he glanced back up at him. "You know, I didn't choose to be your guard. I wanted to head a family group. I have the genetics for it, but Fiona decided on my fate, like she decided yours. She's going to kill me for refusing her. Rhett doesn't mind killing, though. He's made for it."

"Who," Kong asked low. He already knew the answer, but he wanted Kirk to say the vile thing Fiona had ordered. "Who?" he roared.

Kirk's eyes went vacant as he stared at the door from which Layla had disappeared. "Mac."

The room faded around him, and his vision settled to a pinpoint on Kirk's broken eyes. Someone was grabbing his arm.

Kong.

"Kong!" Aviana said, clutching his wrist. "Go to her!" Tears were rimming her eyes as she searched his face. Tiny, dark-haired Aviana. Brave little raven for getting this close to him right now.

His animal roared inside of him, rattling his head and throwing the worried faces around him into uneven vibrations. Kong stumbled forward, lurching toward the door.

Layla. She would be alone now.

He bolted for the parking lot and revved

the engine of his Camaro, then slammed his foot on the gas and spun out of there, spraying gravel behind him. Saratoga's dark streets passed beside him in a blur and, in minutes, he was slamming on the brakes in the Tender Care parking lot. Layla's car was planted at an angle on the curb, her door still open and the engine still running. Kong reached inside and turned it off, then shut her door gently.

The second he stepped through the entrance, he could hear Layla weeping, and asking, "Why?" She chanted over and over she hadn't gotten a chance to say goodbye. He couldn't do this. He couldn't walk in that room and see her destroyed like this. But if he didn't, who would? Who would be strong for her when Mac wasn't around?

Kong's face crumpled the second he walked past the nurses who were crying outside the door. Layla was sitting on the bed, legs curled under her as she cradled Mac's head in her lap. He just looked asleep. Layla's shoulders shook with her weeping, and every word that came murmured from her lips sounded like heartbreak. Kong leaned heavily against the door frame and closed his eyes. Her pain was his fault. He'd known the risk, and he'd pursued her anyway. Sherri stood beside him, gripping his shoulder and wiping her eyes. "It was fast. He just stopped breathing after he took out the tube."

Bullshit. He stopped breathing with a pillow over his face. Rhett had probably smiled as he suffocated him.

Because of him.

Because his fucked up world had collided with the peace Layla had managed to find. After everything she'd been through, she'd been happy with Mac. She'd had as normal a life as she could, and now it had been ripped away from her because Kong had tainted her. He'd put her directly in the crosshairs of Fiona and Rhett, all because he couldn't just let her be.

Some mate he was.

Beaston had said his duty was to make her happy, but this was all he was capable of. Ruining her. Every heartbeat hurt, every movement of his muscles as he sat in the chair next to her and watched his mate break. It took an hour before she'd cried herself out, and when she lay spent, Kong picked her crumpled body up in his arms and strode from the room before she could see the nurses pull the sheet over Mac's face. And as he walked Layla through the front door, something deep within him broke. He could feel himself changing from a cellular level outward. He no longer gave a shit about consequences. This was where the winds of change turned to a fucking hurricane. There was no more cowed Kong, trying to please everyone so that the people he cared about didn't get hurt anymore. He was Kong, dominant death-bringer silverback who had been pushed too far.

Hurting him was one thing, but his people had hurt his mate.

And now they were going to pay with rivers of blood.

****

Layla closed her swollen eyes against the moonlight that streamed through the window of Kong's Camaro. All of the crying had brought on a massive headache.

He's gone.

Another wave of grief threatened to buckle her, so she wrapped her arms more tightly around her middle to keep from falling apart into tiny pieces. She was a broken mirror now. She'd been punched in her middle, and now the jagged shards of her heart were barely holding together.

Kong hadn't said a word the entire way

to…wherever they were going. Maybe he was just driving through the wilderness, she didn't know. Two hours of complete silence had been good for her, though. She needed Kong right now, just like this. Quiet, sitting beside her, ready to hold her in case she fell apart. She wasn't strong right now, but he was cutting a rigid profile.

Strong Kong. Weak Layla.

Mac.

Her family wasn't whole anymore. It had been beautiful for a moment there. Even if it was hard, she'd had Kong and she'd had Mac, and her little make-shift family had felt complete. It had taken her years to build it—to let the right people into her heart—but after a blinding, joyous second, it was over. Dreams broken, and she hadn't gotten to say goodbye.

Kong pulled under a wooden sign over the white gravel road that read *Grayland Mobile Park*.

"What are we doing here?" she asked in a hoarse voice as he pulled in front of a semi-circle of singlewide mobile homes.

Kong didn't say a word as he put the car into park. The driver's side door creaked open, and the car rocked as he got out. With long strides, he walked around the front of the car and opened her door, then reached over, unbuckled her, and pulled her out cradled against his chest.

"You'll be safe here," he murmured. "Ten-ten is magic."

"Ten-ten?" She wrapped her arms around his neck and looked over at the Gray Backs who had filed out of their trailers and gathered in front of them. Faces so somber in the deep shadows of a porch light off one of the trailers, they were almost unfamiliar. She had rarely seen this crew without smiles on their faces.

Willa approached first, her bottom lip trembling as she hugged Layla and Kong. Kong went rigid with Layla in his arms but allowed the affection. It wasn't until after Gia, Georgia, and Easton piled around them, hugging them up tight, that Kong relaxed by a fraction.

Another wave of tears fell from Layla's eyes as she rested her forehead against Willa's. Strange bears and their affection, but it was working. At least she didn't feel numb anymore.

"Can I kill him now?" Easton said in a hard voice.

"No," Kong answered. "I just need you to protect my mate while I take care of some things."

"What things?" Layla asked, voice shaking.

Kong looked down at her with the saddest look. His eyes were still the blazing color of early spring moss, churning like storm clouds. "Mac is dead because of me. You're crying because of me. I can't fix what's been done, but I can avenge him. I can avenge the hurt that's been done to you."

"I don't want you to. I want you to stay with me."

A small smile crept into the corners of Kong's lips. "If I can, I'll come back for you." With that, he lifted his gaze to Creed and settled her on her feet. "Watch over her?"

Creed's dark eyes were somber as he nodded once.

Kong leaned forward and pressed his lips against her forehead. He let them linger there as Layla clutched his shirt in her clenched fists. "I can't lose you, too."

Kong eased back and gripped her arms. The corners of his eyes tightened, and he looked fearsome as he said, "You stay here with the Gray Backs."

And then he released his hold on her and sauntered back to his car without glancing back. The engine of his hotrod roared to life, and Layla stumbled forward as his car faded into the distance the way they'd come.

As his taillights disappeared through the pine forest, a horrible feeling that she was losing the rest of her make-shift family washed over her.

TEN

The hours of driving hadn't cooled Kong's blood. His rage hadn't lessened. He hadn't wised up or conjured second thoughts on the revenge he would take.

Hours of driving had only given him purpose and allowed him to calculate exactly what it was he was doing by going after Rhett.

His people had gone too far, and now Kong would make his stand.

He'd rebelled in his youth when he was a blackback, but Ivan and Gordon had broken him at Fiona's orders. He'd fought and bled and almost died to keep his freedom, but in the end, he'd been too weak to hold it. Things were different now, though. He was fully mature, and he hadn't sat around waiting to be called. He'd focused his energy on building a life, yes, but beyond that, he'd fought anyone who would face off with him in Judge's barn for the sole purpose of never being weak again.

Kong turned onto the black asphalt road that led to his cabin. It was littered with leaves that blew in little tornadoes. In the distance, beyond Damon's mountains, lightning lit up the sky. The air out his open window smelled of ozone and rain. Fitting weather for Mac's passing. Fitting weather for the turmoil within him.

Back at 1010, Layla was probably curled in on herself, crying. The memory of the hopelessness in her eyes as she'd cradled Mac's body slashed through him. Red rage unfurled in his veins as the cabin came into view, a modest one story with huge logs he'd stripped himself. Three bedrooms—one for him and two for the guards who had made his life a living hell. Who had routinely poked and prodded him down a straight path, making all his decisions, keeping him toeing the edge between surviving and actually living. Constantly reminding him his life belonged to Fiona and his seed to a strange family group he hadn't chosen for himself.

Fuck Fiona. Fuck his guards. And fuck some predetermined family group. He was

Layla's—body, soul, bone, and blood.

Rhett had unleashed something inside of Kong that couldn't be caged again. He'd awoken a monster.

Rhett stood from a rocking chair on the porch, a cruel smile twisted on his lips and an excited glint in his blazing silver eyes.

Kong pulled his car in front of the cabin and parked it, then slid out and said, "You went too far."

"No such thing," Rhett murmured. His eye twitched, and he smelled of fur. "See, that was always the problem with you, Kong. You had this moral compass that weakened you. You're a fucking silverback. You don't have to tiptoe around ethics. We *take* what we want," Rhett gritted out, clenching his fist in front of him. "We *do* what we want, and you know why? Because everyone else is beneath us. And what did you do? You made friends with bears and falcons and ravens. With *humans*. You, the Lowlander Silverback, fucking royalty and destined to father the next generation of highborn gorillas, and you befriended bottom feeders." Rhett spat. "I should've been the Kong."

"If Fiona's idea of the Kong is a silverback who murders on command, then perhaps you should've been. Weak?" Kong shook his head slow. "You do everything she says, no questions asked, at the cost of your soul, and you call me weak." Kong lifted his chin. "You're the bottom feeder, Rhett. Begging for scraps, guarding a silverback you hate because Fiona said his dick is important. You're a glorified cock blocker turned murderer. Tell me, did it make you feel good to kill an innocent old man? Did it make you feel strong to overpower a human on his deathbed?"

"Shut up."

"Do you feel proud that you've done what your master told you to?"

"I said shut up!" Rhett paced the porch. "You're wrong. Fiona respects me. She trusts me to do the things others are too weak to. I'm her right-hand man."

Kong huffed a humorless, single laugh. "You stupid, blind fuck. Fiona respects no one."

"You're wrong! I pay my dues, and a family group is as good as mine someday."

"And why would she give you females, Rhett? Why would she give a guard dog her prized possessions?"

Rhett linked his hands behind his head and narrowed his eyes. "I know what you're doing. You're trying to get in my head. Trying to get me to betray my own people."

"No, Rhett. I don't care about getting in your head, and I don't care if you betray anyone. Your life is over after tonight. Can you hear your heartbeat pounding in your chest? I can. Enjoy it now because the sound won't last for long. Listen," Kong said on a breath. Even over the breeze of the oncoming storm, he could make it out. "Bum-bum, bum-bum. So fast. So scared because you can see it in my eyes. Your death is coming, and I'm the grim fucking reaper."

Rhett's smile stretched his face into something feral. "A challenge from the mighty Kong?"

Kong dipped his chin once.

"All over a human. Did you know," Rhett said, pulling his shirt over his head, "old Mac knew why I was there the second I slipped in his window? He tried to yell for help but I was faster."

Kong shook his head, warding off the black inky tendrils of rage that were pushing against his insides. "Stop it."

"He yelled under the pillow. Little. Pathetic. Human sounds. I took a picture for Fiona. She likes to see bodies."

Kong's skin exploded with a ripping sound

and a volley of cracking bones that echoed across the clearing. He slammed his oversize fists against the ground, shaking the earth. Rhett's silverback burst from him and charged. Kong beat his chest, the sound popping like a drum before he lowered to all fours and ran for Rhett.

He was going to bleed him, rip him, kill him for hurting his mate. For hurting Mac. They clashed with a force of an eighteen-wheeler head-on collision. This wasn't posturing like so many gorilla battles were. This wasn't beating the chest and circling before one decided he was beat on dominance alone and slunk away. This was a rip-roaring, bloodletting, fur-ripping, skin-hacking, body-beating battle to the grave. The woods were filled with the death chants of their roaring.

Kong hacked at him with his long, razor-sharp teeth, beating Rhett with his arms, pummeling him toward the trees. Rhett turned and swung from a low branch to buy time, but Kong was right on him. On the ground or in the trees, it made no difference. Rhett would breathe his last breath tonight for what he'd taken from Layla.

The beast Kong didn't think, wasn't careful, didn't calculate. Rhett had raised the monster within him, and now he'd have to deal with the consequences. No chance for control, he let his gorilla have his mind. Rhett was on the run now. Kong could see fear in his eyes when he looked behind him to see how close Kong was. He swung from branch to branch, higher and higher, but the canopy wouldn't save him. A thick branch cracked under the force as Kong launched himself toward Rhett. His body crashed into the silverback, who screamed as his fingers brushed and missed his next branch. They tumbled to the forest floor and slammed onto the unforgiving ground. Kong reared up and roared, exposing his long canines so that Rhett could see his end coming, then he slammed his hands down. Rhett went limp under the force of his fists, but movement through the trees said this wasn't over yet.

He smelled them then, Ivan and Gordon. His own personal nightmares. The silverbacks who had taken such pleasure in carrying out Fiona's task of breaking him and threatening his mother. They were here for round two.

Ivan was Changed already, but Gordon was still human, and he was smiling in the blue moonlight. "Very good, Kong."

Kong lifted his lip and charged a few steps.

A warning. *Back off or you're next.*

"Fiona will be glad to see how far you've come."

Gordon reeked of dominance. The smell raised the short hairs on the back of Kong's thick neck.

"We're here to bring you in." Gordon tossed a look at Rhett's body, then flicked his attention back to Kong. "Fiona thought Rhett wouldn't be able to neutralize you by himself, and Kirk is next to worthless. It seems our wise leader was right. Come on, boy. Your destiny awaits."

"Fuck you," Kong said in a growly, inhuman voice, a voice that was marred by his animal vocal cords.

Gordon's eyes tightened as Ivan paced beside him, his clenched fists punching the earth. "Don't do this again. Remember the last time you fought your title? So much agony. So much blood."

Slowly, Kong stepped over Rhett's body and lifted his head, puffing out his chest as he stood ready. His lips twitched with rage as he glared down the shifters who had stolen his freedom.

Whether he liked it or not, this was the moment Kong chose. This wasn't just about avenging Mac anymore. This was the moment he declared Layla was his and cut himself off from his people completely. There would be no chance at redemption in Fiona's eyes if he killed her prized enforcers.

This was the moment he took his life back or died trying.

With a quick drum of his chest, Kong charged the silverbacks.

And then there was pain.

ELEVEN

Layla carefully crawled over Willa's sleeping form in the queen-size bed. She and Georgia had stayed late into the night, soothing her heartache, and had fallen asleep beside her. Layla, however, was still wide awake with worry.

Kong should be back by now.

She walked through the small singlewide, her bare feet cold against the cheap laminate wood flooring. There were squishy parts and creaks, but she made it to the living room with its clean, white panel walls. She pulled a thick blanket off the back of the green couch and let herself out the front door as quietly as she could.

The first streaks of dawn ghosted the horizon. She sat in a rocking chair on the sprawling cedar porch off the side of the trailer and huddled into the blanket. The tears on her cheeks had dried in the middle of the night, and now, she felt drained, as if she had nothing left but worry over Kong. She didn't know how long she sat there waiting. Perhaps it was ten minutes, perhaps an hour. The sky lightened to a soft gray that met dark storm clouds, and still, she kept her eyes trained on the road. He would come back to her. He had to. Fate surely wasn't so cruel that it would take both of the men from her life in one night.

Movement caught her attention, and she unfolded her legs and padded toward the porch railing. Her shoulders sagged with disappointment. Not Kong. It was Matt, Willa's mate. His sandy hair was disheveled as if he hadn't slept a wink either, and his bright blue eyes swam with worry as he paced near a jacked-up Chevy truck. He muttered, "Come on, Kong," then hit a button on his phone and lifted it to his ear. "Where are you?" Matt settled with his back to her, staring at the road she'd been watching. He muttered a curse and yanked the phone away from his ear. "You coming or what?" he asked without turning around.

"Y-yes."

"Get in," he clipped out, casting her a

bright-eyed glance over his shoulder.

Layla draped the blanket over the railing and made her way to his truck as quietly as she could. Then she climbed in through his side and settled onto the passenger's seat.

"Whatever happens—"

"He's fine," she said in a hard voice.

Matt inhaled deeply and nodded his head once. Then he jammed the engine and slammed his foot on the gas, spinning out as he sped off down the road.

"Kong's your friend," she whispered numbly as she watched the towering pines blur by the window.

"He's my best friend. He kept me sane before Willa came along. Kong bought me time until she found me. Layla?"

"Hmm?"

"I'm sorry about your dad."

She didn't have the heart to tell him Mac wasn't her real father. He felt like it anyway. "Thanks."

"I don't remember mine."

She jerked her gaze to Matt and frowned. "How old were you when he died?"

"He didn't die. Or maybe he did, I don't know. I was taken from my parents young. Look, what Rhett did...he didn't do that because he's a shifter. He did it because he is a murderous asshole."

"I know."

Matt dared a glance at her, then returned his attention back to the road. "I just didn't want you thinking all shifters are like that."

She offered him an understanding smile, then sighed and drew her knees up to her chest. Matt turned on the music a few minutes later to drown out the silence of the cab, but not even the soft notes of country love songs could settle the nerves in her stomach. She knew what she could and couldn't handle, and she was on the brink now. If anything happened to Kong…

She swallowed hard and blinked back tears. Mac was gone, and now Kong was everything good in her life.

And he should've been back by now.

The drive stretched on and on, suffocating her slowly until she cracked the window for some fresh air and relief. Matt did the same, and when he looked at her, his eyes were churning light silver. He gripped the wheel until his knuckles turned white as he drove down a black asphalt road that looked newly poured. Storm clouds roiled over them, threatening to unleash a shower of pelting rain at any moment. Kong's car sat at an angle in front of a cabin. Cedar logs and a green roof with a wraparound porch. This place was beautiful. She would've dreamed of living here with Kong someday if it weren't for the blood trailing up the porch stairs and into the front door.

A soft growl came from Matt, and his nostrils flared as he scented the air. "Stay here."

"No," she rasped, forcing the word past her tightening throat. "I have to see."

Matt waited for her to exit the car and took her hand before he led her, angled behind his wide shoulders, toward the cabin. This moment right here was completely surreal. Her legs were floating across the grass and wild flowers. Pink and orange and yellow. And Red. Grass dyed crimson. Burgundy speckles on the delicate petals, and little by little Matt's grip tightened around her hand until it should've hurt. Her bones ground together, but she couldn't feel anything. There was blood on the toes of her boots, glossy red on matte black.

A man met them at the door, startling her to a stop on the porch, her legs splayed over a dark smear. He was tall and lean. Black hair gone silver at the temples with dark eyes and a young face. He wore dark gray dress pants and a button-up white collared shirt. Red on white. Red on his hands as he wiped them over and over with a ruined washcloth.

"Damon," Matt said in a choked voice. "Where is he?"

"He needs time."

"Does he live?"

Damon nodded his chin once. "There were three of them."

"Fuck." Matt's voice shook. "Bodies?"

Damon's lips turned up in a thin, wry smile. "Gone. Is this her? Mate of the Kong?"

Matt pulled Layla from behind and pushed her in front of him, hands clamped tightly around her shoulders. "This is Layla."

Damon studied her with black, bottomless eyes that would miss nothing. At last, he placed his hands behind his back and bowed slightly. "It's an honor to meet you."

"The honor is mine," she whispered. Damon Daye, owner of the mountains, protector of the shifters. The last immortal dragon if rumors were true. And apparently, he'd had a hand in helping Kong. "Can I see him?"

Damon looked troubled, but stepped aside

to let her pass. She followed the red to an open door. There was a hand print smeared onto the white paint, and a phone lay on the wooden floor. The screen of the discarded cell phone was covered in sticky fingerprints.

Kong lay on his side in the bed, skin clean but covered in stitches. His chest rose and fell slowly, a soft rattling sound ending each breath. He cracked his eyes open. Green and inhuman. Beautiful. Layla covered her mouth with her hands, and her shoulders shook with the relieved sob that wrenched from her throat. He was alive. Barely, but it counted.

"You stitched him?" Matt asked low.

"I didn't have a choice," Damon said. "He'd lost too much blood by the time I got to him, and he wasn't healing like he should've been. He was wide open—"

A long rattling growl sounded from Kong as he blinked and dragged a warning gaze to Damon.

Damon cleared his throat. "Come on, Matt. Let's give them a moment."

The sound of scuffling shoes faded away as she approached the bed. Kneeling beside him, she held his hand. "You silly monkey, what have you done?" Her voice was nothing but a wisp of air as she smiled at him through her tears.

"Mac is avenged," he said hoarsely. "Rhett's dead."

"Damon said there were three."

"Fiona sent the silverbacks that had broken me."

"Kong," she whispered in horror, her heart aching for him.

"It's over now." He squeezed her hand in a much stronger grip than she'd expected. "I'm not leaving you, Layla. I'm here now, in this. I'll fight for us. I'm going to keep you safe."

Layla's face crumpled as she nuzzled her cheek against his hand. "You scared me last night. I thought...I thought I lost you, too."

He grunted an inhuman sound and gripped the back of her neck. Pulling gently, he guided her onto the bed next to him. Fists curled in against his chest, she lay her head in the cradle of his arm.

"I have this vision of us now," he whispered against her ear. "I imagine you holding our firstborn. I imagine you laughing and looking at me just like you were looking at me now. Like I'm everything. You're all the family I need, Layla." He let his lips linger on her cheek. "I love you more than my own life. I'm not going anywhere."

As another tear slipped from the corner of her eye and dampened the pillow underneath, she smiled and relaxed against him. She wouldn't deal with Mac's loss alone. Kong would be here until she was strong again.

He'd chosen *her*.

He loved *her*.

He'd sacrificed himself for *her*.

Layla pressed her hand over his heartbeat, thrumming steady and strong—a song that was pivotal to her existence now.

No matter what came after this, they would face it together.

TWELVE

There was a break in the rain just long enough for Mac's funeral. Layla lifted her eyes to the sunrays coming down on the valley beyond the cemetery and smiled. Maybe that was Mac, telling her that he was with his Gloria again, and that everything would be okay.

Kong watched her intently as the casket was lowered into the ground. Mac's service had been touching in the most surprising ways. She thought it would be a small funeral, but half the town had shown up. She wasn't doing this alone as she'd feared. She had Kong beside her and the Gray Backs in a somber line behind her. Willa stood on her other side, holding her hand and dabbing her eyes. Jake stood across the lowering, glossed mahogany casket with a sympathetic smile. Barney was here, and even Jackson had shown up to pay his respects. The nurses were all here, and beside a tree in the distance, Kirk leaned against the trunk, dressed in a black suit like Kong's. The Ashe Crew and the Boarlanders had come, too, and this morning when she'd checked her mail, there was a postcard from Mom and Dad saying how sorry they were about Mac passing. She'd put it up on the fridge with the others.

The funeral-goers drifted back to their cars, but Kong and the Gray Backs stayed with her until the casket hit dirt. Mac was buried by his Gloria now, just like he'd always wanted. And in a few days, when they laid sod over his grave, Layla would come out and water the grass and put fresh flowers on their headstones because that's what made her feel close to them. Cemeteries weren't for the dead. They were for the living so they could still feel connected to their loved ones somehow.

"You ready to go home?" Kong asked low.

Home. She frowned at the stream of people clad in black who were walking down the hill toward the line of cars below. She hadn't ever felt at home in her apartment, and Kong's cabin wasn't home. 1010 was safe and comfortable, but three days and three nights wasn't long enough for a place to feel like home. The only home that meant anything was Mac's house, but that was going to be sold at auction.

Everything felt so different now, off-kilter and strange, as if it wasn't really her life, but someone else's. She was mated to Kong, and she'd fallen heart-first into the Gray Back Crew who had been there for her in such unexpected ways over the last few days. In a matter of a week, everything real in her old life had disappeared, and everything else had drawn up into fine focus.

Kong was still waiting on her answer with a worried look in his soft brown eyes.

She smiled and nodded, then followed him toward his Camaro. His gait hitched slightly, thanks to a broken bone that hadn't been reset in time, but other than that and a map of scars across his body, he had healed.

He opened her door and waited until she was inside, then he draped his suit jacket over her legs. While they followed the Gray Backs' work trucks up the winding mountain roads, Kong's hand stayed around hers, big and strong, steadying the shake in her fingers. His profile struck her as beautiful with the trees passing by and the storm clouds muting the light against his skin. High cheek bones, dark eyes to match dark brows to match dark hair he'd styled in a sexy, messy look today. His skin was tan compared to the white dress shirt that clung to his muscular shoulders. The top button was unbuttoned, and his black dress pants pressed against his powerful legs as he pushed down the gas on his rumbling hotrod.

Mine.

She smiled when her attention drifted to the Grayland Mobile Park sign over the white gravel road. It was a relief to drive under it, though she couldn't pinpoint why. Perhaps because nothing bad had happened here. There were no memories of Mac to haunt her like there were down in Saratoga. Stepping out of the car, she waved at Willa, Georgia, and Aviana who held down the hems of their black dresses as they scurried to their trailers with their mates.

Creed pulled little Rowan from her car seat and cradled her tightly against his chest, cooing as she fussed. Leaves swirled around his feet as he looked up with his ink-colored eyes, so much like Damon's. "You tell us if you need anything," he said to her before he turned to a waiting Gia and walked away with his daughter cuddled in his arms.

Kong's fingertips were light as a feather against her lower back as he guided her up the porch stairs of 1010. He'd gone quiet lately. Dimmer. Like a lantern that was almost out of oil and struggling to stay lit. Mac's death and the battle that followed weighed heavily on him.

"It's not your fault, you know?" she murmured as she stepped into the bedroom and slipped out of her heels.

"Mmm," Kong said noncommittally.

She unbuttoned his shirt slowly. "It's not."

Kong went still under her touch, his eyes somber as he stared at her. "I wanted things to be different." His nose and lip twitched, a sign of the animal that lived beneath his skin. He did that when he was thinking hard about something. "I wish we could've dated, like other people. Movies, dinner, picnics...normal shit. Not all this heaviness. I didn't want it to be a loss that bonded us, Layla."

She smiled and pushed his shirt off his shoulders. "It wasn't. I wanted you long before any of this stuff happened.

She untucked the hem of his white undershirt and lifted it over his head. He grunted as he lifted his arms. Healed he might be, but there were still aching nerves nestled in the deepest wounds. She traced a long pair of scars across his ribs with a light touch.

"Beautiful mate," she whispered. "I don't know how I would've gotten through this week without you."

Kong gripped her wrist as she got too close to a wide cavern of uneven red scar tissue under his arm. "You wouldn't have had to go through this week if it weren't for me."

"Mac had cancer, Kong."

His grip loosened as he searched her eyes.

"It's why he was in hospice. It had spread, and the doctors couldn't do anything. If it weren't for you and the Gray Backs, I would've planned his funeral alone and stood for him at that gravesite alone a couple of months from now. I would've mourned alone. I hate Rhett for what he did, and Kong, there are times where I wish I could've watched you rip him apart." Her words shook like a lit candle wick in a strong wind. "But, mate," she whispered, cupping his cheek. "It was Mac's time, no matter what you or I wished. It was Fiona and Rhett's awful decision that had nothing—*nothing*—to do with you. I don't blame you, and it hurts me to see you blaming yourself."

Kong's chest rose with his deep inhalation,

and he leaned his cheek into her palm, making a raspy sound with his two-day scruff. She leaned up on tiptoes and kissed his lips. Then she turned and pulled her hair aside, watching him in the dresser mirror.

A slow smile spread across his lips as he unzipped her dress slowly.

"I have a boner to pick with you, mister."

Kong chuckled deeply, and she closed her eyes to revel in the sound of it. Damn, she'd missed that over the past few days. Now, it was medicine for her soul.

"I think the saying goes 'I have a bone to pick with you.'"

"No, boner, because you have shown no interest in sleeping with me."

"The couch is comfortable, and I wanted to give you space." Kong unsnapped her bra, then reached his hands through her open dress and slid his touch around her ribs until he cupped her breasts.

"That's not what I'm talking about," she said on a breath.

"Oh, I know what you're talking about, woman." His words were a rattling growl that lifted gooseflesh across her forearms.

"Then why haven't you made love to me?"

Kong pressed his lips against the back of

her neck and sucked gently. Curling back against him, she sighed. He worked his way down the side of her throat and grazed his teeth right over the mark he'd given her before everything went wrong.

"Because you're in heat," he whispered against her skin. "I can smell it. Practically taste it on the air." He rocked his hips against her back, pressing his hard, thick erection against her. "You think I haven't wanted to cover you? Wrong. It's hard to think about anything else, but it didn't seem like the right time to talk about family planning." He gripped her long hair at the base of her neck and lifted, exposing the other side to his biting, sucking affection.

"You're ready for a baby?" she asked. "With me?"

Kong spun her and settled her hips onto the dresser, then pulled the front of her dress off her arms and let it pile in her lap. He locked his arms on either side of her hips and took a sip of her lips. His eyes weren't soft and brown anymore. They were the wild green color. "I am. I told you I want a family. It happens when silverbacks mature. I've set up a life here, a business, so I could afford to take care of a family. My instincts scream every time I smell those sexy pheromones you're putting out. *Cover her. Put a baby in her. Make a family with her.* It gets overwhelming, but the timing isn't right, and you don't have the same instincts to breed as I do. I want to get you pregnant, yes. But I also want you happy, and I want our love story to be that slow burn like Mac's was with his Gloria. I never want you resenting me for pushing you into something this big so fast. So I'll wait. We'll be careful and use protection until you're ready."

She cupped his neck and grinned. "You want to know something?"

"Hmm?" he asked, leaning down and drawing one of her nipples into his mouth.

She moaned and arched her back to give him a better angle. "I really...really...*really* like that you want a family with me, and only me. Oh!"

Kong sucked hard and dragged his lips across her chest to draw her other nipple into his mouth. She spread her legs wider to give him more access. She had to get this out before she lost her mind completely. "But I think you're right. I want to be your family group, and I want to give you a baby, but with everything going on right now, I think we should wait until the dust clears." Panting, she lifted his chin until his gaze hooked onto hers. "I'm on the pill now, but when we're ready, I'll stop taking it. Until then, we can have fun practicing."

And Kong, that sexy as hell man, didn't even make her feel guilty for putting off a family—not for a second. He gave her a wicked smile and dropped to his knees, then rucked up her dress, exposing the thin black lacies she'd worn to hide a panty line in her dress. "Perfect," he murmured before he looked back up at her with his blazing green eyes. "You want me to make you forget?"

Oh, she knew what he was offering. A chance to forget the muck of the last few days. He was offering to lift the heavy weight off her chest for a little while—to give her a break from the darkness that had inched into her life like a suffocating fog.

"Yes." She couldn't say it fast enough. She'd needed this kind of affection, but Kong had seemed reluctant to give it lately. Now that she knew it was for her benefit and not because he didn't want it, she couldn't get him inside her fast enough. The soft rip of her panties filled the room, and she leaned the back of her head against the mirror as Kong lowered a hungry gaze between her legs and let off a soft growl.

"Eat me," she pleaded desperate to lose herself with him.

He pulled the backs of her knees until she was at the edge of the dresser, then he gripped her hips and leaned forward, pressing soft lips against her slick folds. A tease.

"Please," she whispered, rolling her hips forward.

He pulled her clit between his lips and sucked gently. In shaking gasps, Layla's breath left her body as she ran her fingers through his hair, then gripped it hard. Punishment for his teasing. The growl in his throat grew louder and vibrated against her right where she was most sensitive. She bowed against him and groaned. Maybe she really was in heat, or the human equivalent, because right now, she was unbelievably sensitive. She closed her eyes and imagined his long dick sliding into her. Kong released her clit and drove his tongue into her, drawing a gasp from her lips. His fingers dug into her waist, but it didn't hurt. She wanted him rough this time. *Forget. Forget everything.*

Kong angled his head as she raked her fingernails through his hair and pulled him closer. He went deeper the next time he pushed into her, and she spread her legs and cried out. He'd found his rhythm now, not too fast, not too slow, careful to pay attention to her clit every few strokes. Her legs were going numb. Hell, her whole body was floating as he pushed her closer to release.

"No, no, no," she murmured. "Want more. Want you inside of me. Want you to cover me." Yes, that sounded right. Like he called it. Like his people called it. Breeding. Covering. Wild, like her Kong.

With a growl, Kong sucked her clit hard and then stood, tugging her dress over her head in one smooth motion. Kong pulled her off the dresser, then settled her stomach on the edge of the bed, feet on the floor. "Lock your legs," he rumbled out. "Ass in the air for me, beautiful."

The jingle of his belt as he removed it brought a wave of excited anticipation as she arched her back and gave him a full view of her soaking wet sex.

His teeth grazed her skin just above her ass, and then his kisses worked their way up until his mouth was at the mark he'd given her. The head of his hard cock was right there, pressing into her by an inch. When he eased out, she wanted to scream. He pushed into her a little farther, and her legs relaxed. She moaned and rocked her hips with him the next time. He took her deeply. God, he was long and thick. Stretching. Almost pain, but more pleasure.

"Harder," she said on a panting breath.

Kong grabbed her breast, other arm locked against the bed beside her ribcage. With a grunt, he thrust in until she'd taken all of him. His body was rigid, tensed, muscles firing and twitching as he pushed into her again and again. "Layla," he gritted out in a helpless voice. Yes. Yes! She closed her eyes against the primal growl that rattled from his chest against her back.

"Harder," she begged.

His powerful hips jerked as he slammed into her. His hand was rough on her breast, but she didn't care. She wanted him like this. She'd been wrong to tell him to be gentle with her when they'd first met. Kong wasn't a gentle man. He was rough and feral, and she loved that about him. She shouldn't have stifled him. It was she who needed to compromise and accept his animal. And his animal liked to fuck. Hard. She gasped as he slammed into her faster. She was so wet. Could feel it every time he slid into her. Slick sound. Slick shaft. God, he felt so good inside of her.

The snarl in his throat grew louder. Almost there. The pressure filled her entire body, from her middle to her fingertips. She arched her back as he gripped her hair and clamped his teeth onto her shoulder. Not hard enough to break the skin, but hard enough to draw the first pulse of a body-shattering orgasm from her. Kong froze on the next stroke with her name rasping from his lips. Jets of heat shot into her, and he bucked into her again and again, matching her orgasm. With one last growl, he pushed her chest onto the bed and pumped into her again where he stayed locked deep inside of her, emptying himself completely. His body relaxed against her as he kissed the back of her neck, over and over.

"I love you. I love you," she chanted in a whisper because it felt so important that he knew right now.

He smiled against her skin and bit her softly again. Sexy. Bitey. Kong. With a sigh, he slid out of her and pulled her flush against him on the bed. He spread the covers over their legs and kissed her softly. It wasn't the passionate kisses they sometimes had when they were overwhelmed with each other. This one said those three important words back to her without any sound. He cupped the back of her head like she was precious and sipped her until she smiled sleepily and hugged him close.

He inhaled deeply and pulled her body close as he rested his chin on top of her head. "Thanks for forgiving me," he murmured so softly she almost missed it.

Shaking her head against the soft pillow, she said, "There was nothing to forgive."

And as she traced the scars on his body, the ones he'd received avenging Mac and choosing her, she was struck with how lucky she was to be in this moment. Wrapped in the arms of the man she loved. A week ago, this wasn't a possibility, but here she was.

And suddenly, Kong's earlier question took on a new meaning.

You ready to go home?

Home wasn't a place anymore.

She smiled against his skin and kissed a scar right above his heart.

Home was Kong.

THIRTEEN

Kong's cell phone rattled across the bedside table, kept from falling off the edge only by the cord that was charging it. He scrubbed his hands over his face and squinted at the glowing caller ID on the screen. Five in the morning, and why the hell would Kirk be calling him this early, or at all? Kong hadn't talked to him since the night Fiona had given the order to kill Mac.

He accepted the call and murmured, "Hang on." Then he looked over at Layla who was still sleeping peacefully beside him, her arm thrown over his middle and a slight frown drawing down her delicately arched, sandy-blond eyebrows. No make-up and clad in nothing but a pair of cotton panties and a tank top, and damn his mate stole his breath away.

He slipped out from under her arm and

pulled the covers over her, tucking her in tightly before he unhooked the phone from the charger and padded out of the trailer.

"What do you want?" he asked low as he leaned on the front porch railing. The Gray Backs would be up soon to go to work on the landing, but he didn't want to perk up their oversensitive hearing and make them lose any sleep.

"I just got a call from Fiona."

Kong's heartbeat stuttered and then picked up double time.

"Kong, she's not done coming after you and Layla."

"Why would you tell me this? Aren't you one of her henchmen?"

"No." Kirk's voice sounded off. Defeated or disillusioned, perhaps. "I'm already dead, Kong. I have been since she gave the order to take out Mac. I was supposed to help Rhett, but I didn't. Couldn't."

"I thought you were playing watch out while Rhett—"

Kirk made a clicking sound behind his teeth, and static blasted across the phone as if he had rubbed the speaker against his shirt. "I told you I didn't choose to be your guard. This is a courtesy call. I'm handling the sawmill until you're ready to take it over again. I just wanted to say you don't have to worry about the business. I've got this until she comes for me. It's the least I can do for what I was a part of."

"But you said you weren't a part of Mac's death."

"That's not what I'm talking about. I mean for what I've had to do to you. Controlling you, watching you, berating every little thing you did wrong. You didn't do anything wrong, Kong. You're still not doing anything wrong. Our people are fucked up. Fucked. Up. I told Fiona I'm rogue now, but before I did, she asked where you were staying. I didn't tell her anything, but she'll find you. She asked me what happened to Gordon and Ivan. To Rhett. She said they hadn't called or come home. I didn't answer, but that was answer enough for her, you know?"

"Kirk, you didn't have to go rogue for me."

"It wasn't for you, man. It was for me. I want my pride intact at the end. Besides, Fiona has no use for me anymore. She won't give me a family group, and I suck at murdering people for her. I just wanted to warn you it isn't over with her yet."

Kong slammed his fist onto the railing and

ran his hands through his sleep-mussed hair. "I don't get it. Why this obsession with me? It can't just be the birthmark. Why can't she just let me go?"

"Don't you see? It *is* the birthmark. Every generation sired by the silverback with the mark of the Kong has gone down in our history books as the strongest. The smartest. The ones who made a difference in our survival. It isn't you. It's your genetics she needs."

"Needs?"

"Kong, the family group she's put together for you? She's in it. She's the head female."

Shock slammed into him, stealing his breath away. No. "Fiona wants to breed?" She was forty and still capable, but she'd only ever shown interest in ruling the gorilla shifters.

"Yeah, man. But she won't bear offspring for just anyone. She wants you to father her get. She wants her offspring in the history books."

A hundred things snapped into place. Fiona searching tirelessly for him after his mother had stolen him away. Her putting so much effort into breaking him when he was a blackback. Her obsession with the contract and not allowing him to taint his seed. It wasn't for the betterment of a family group. It was because he was being groomed to be her claim.

His stomach curdled with a gritty, nauseous feeling as he sank onto the cedar floorboards, his back against the railing. "Holy shit," he murmured, shaking his head in disbelief. If this was true, she would never give up, and Layla would never be safe.

Kirk swallowed audibly over the line. "Anyway. I just wanted to give you a heads up. I actually like Layla for you. Can you tell her..." His voice cracked, and he cleared his throat and tried again. "Can you tell her I'm sorry about Mac?"

Mac's death wasn't Kirk's fault, but he got it. He'd been blaming himself for the better part of a week now, too. "Yeah. I will."

"I'll be at the sawmill if you need me," Kirk said. "For backup or whatever. My days are numbered, so for the rest of them, I'm good with making up for what I've had to push you into all these years. I'd better go. We have a few orders to fill today."

"All right, man. Kirk?" Kong asked before he could hang up.

"Yeah?"

"It's okay. What you had to do? It's *okay*."

Kirk was quiet for a long time before he said, "It's not, but thanks for saying that. Goodbye, Kong."

The line went dead, and Kong rested his head back against the railing and stared at Layla's bedroom window.

He'd thought this was over, but the scars on his body were just the warm-up.

Layla wasn't any safer now than she had been before he'd challenged Rhett and the others.

****

When Layla woke up, Kong was sitting on the edge of the bed with his back to her. She slid her hand up the uneven skin of his back, over the bumps and ridges of the scars she had now memorized with her touch. Over the long, dark shape of the birthmark that had almost come between them.

"Good morning," she murmured sleepily.

He looked over his shoulder with a ready smile, but his eyes were green.

"What's wrong?"

"I want to take you on a date."

She ducked her face and hid her flattered smile as butterflies fluttered away in her stomach. "Where?"

"Willa told me about this bait shop she

sells worms to. She said the owner just expanded and added a barbeque joint onto it for the tourists who fish up here. It's only half an hour away, so we wouldn't have to make another drive all the way into Saratoga for me to take you out."

She angled her face and frowned. "Why are your eyes glowing?"

His smile faded slowly, and he shook his head. "No reason." But his voice sounded off, hollow, as if he didn't believe in the words enough to put force behind them.

"Okay."

"Okay?"

"Yes, I'll go on a date with you. Silly monkey," she said through a giggle, "you'll talk about starting a family with me, no problem, but you get nervous asking me out?" She bit her lip against the smile that cracked her face wide open. Then she jumped up and climbed on his back like a koala bear. Wrapping her legs around his middle, she said, "Take me to the shower, silly monkey. I want to get pretty for our date."

Kong chuckled and bit her arm gently. "As you command, my queen."

"Mmm," she said, laying kisses along the tense muscles of his neck. "I like that. You can use that nickname whenever you want.

It was late in the morning, and she couldn't believe how long she'd slept, but perhaps she'd needed the sleep. Maybe her heart and head had needed a break from thinking and grieving. Even though her chest still felt heavy with Mac's loss, she felt better this morning than she had since he'd passed.

She bit his ear playfully before he leaned over with her weight still on his back. He turned on the hot tap and shimmied out of his cotton sleep pants that were light blue and thin enough she could always see his morning wood through the material. The kind that hung low on his hips and showed off those two yummy strips of muscle that wrapped around his waist. "Sexy mate," she murmured, slipping from his back.

"I like that nickname."

"Mate of many muscles." She peeled off her shirt and wiggled her boobies at him when she caught him looking.

"Mmm, keep going."

"Not *the* Kong anymore. *My* Kong."

"That's the one," he said through a dazzling smile as his eyes faded to muddy green. "That's my favorite."

He lifted her off the bath mat and wrapped

her legs around his waist as he stepped into the shower. He pressed her back against the plastic shower wall and slid into her slowly, eyes on her. Always on her. This wasn't about covering her, or pheromones. It wasn't about practicing for a family. Something in Kong's soul was aching, and he needed her. His eyes dimmed to the soft brown she'd fallen in love with over the years. He dipped in to kiss her, only to ease back and watch her face again as he stroked slowly into her. And when they were both close, he rested his forehead against hers and whispered that he loved her. And when he'd met her orgasm with one of his own, he pulled every pulsing aftershock from her, then slid out and washed her body as if she was a goddess. As though she truly was his queen.

He kept her off balance as the morning faded to afternoon. Playful, happy, serious, troubled, playful again. He carried her over his shoulder and gripped her ass through her sundress on the way to his Camaro.

Willa and Gia waved to them as they pulled away, and Layla beamed. "I like it here."

"Yeah?" he asked, pulling her fingertips to his lips as he drove away from the trailer park.

"I know we have to go back to Saratoga

soon, but that place made everything easier. The people there and the woods."

"Ten-ten."

"Yeah."

"Told you it was magic."

"You. You've made everything okay."

He threw her a questioning glance, and there it was again. The speckles of green, just starting to glow like fireflies in his gaze. He rasped his newly shaved jaw across her knuckles but didn't say anything as he dragged his gaze back to the road and slid on a pair of sunglasses.

"Would you be mad if I put my feet on the dashboard?" she asked, slipping her feet from her sandals and wiggling her toes right over the finely detailed glove box.

"Maybe."

"You know, if I make footprints, you'll always think of me when you get in and see them."

He ghosted a glance at the dashboard, then nodded his head. "Do it. I like thinking about you."

"Really?" She was shocked to her bones. Kong loved his car.

"Really." He pressed her knee so her left foot touched the warm dash. "Leave your mark on here, woman."

So she did. She rested her feet there the entire drive to Moosey's Bait and Barbecue. When she took them off in the parking lot, the dash still looked pretty shiny, but if she squinted and looked hard at just the right angle, there were two faint smudges, and that was good enough. "Now, if anything ever happens to me, you'll still have a part of me with you in the passenger's seat." Ugh. Where had that morbid thought come from?

Kong stared at the prints too long after putting the Camaro into park.

"Did you change your mind? I can polish it again." Layla turned and reached for the detailing wipes he kept in the back seat.

"No," he rushed out. "I like them. Leave them." He leaned over and kissed her. Just a sweet sip with a gentle smack at the end, and then he was getting out of the car, leaving her off-balance as he'd done all morning.

Kong was a tall glass of arctic water on a hot day. His legs were long, lean, and powerful against the hole-riddled jeans that clung to his waist just right. The thin V-neck white T-shirt that hung over his defined chest was enough to draw a gulp from her lips. Aviator sunglasses hid his eyes, and scars peeked out from under the neck of his shirt. He was rocking that sexy, clean-shaven jaw that was sharp as glass with thick, dark hair styled longer on top and, holy hotness, she couldn't believe he was hers.

Hers in all the ways that mattered. Her mate. Her love and, someday, he would be the father of her children. Over the past week, he had held baby Rowan anytime Gia and Creed would let him, and Layla had fallen in love with the way he looked at the infant. A tiny baby cradled so gently against his chest as he rocked slowly back and forth and talked to her. Kong would make a great father and teammate to raise a family with. She'd never admitted it to anyone other than Mac, but she wanted lots of kids. She'd grown up lonely, confused by the definition of family, but with Kong, she could have something special—a sense of belonging that filled the hungry hole in her heart.

He opened her door and held out his hand. "You ready, beautiful?"

Grinning, she slid her palm against his and allowed him to help her out of the car. "You know, I always imagined what it would be like if you asked me out. I would see you at the bar and daydream about what you would say and where you would take me."

"Disappointed?"

"Not at all. Being with you is better than I could've imagined."

His throat moved as he swallowed hard. She wished she could see his eyes, but all she could see was her own smiling reflection in his sunglasses. Turning, he linked his fingers with hers and led her into Moosey's.

Barbecue sandwiches and sodas ordered, they picked a seat outside on the picnic table farthest away from the lunch rush. There was a red and white checkered umbrella spread open above them, shielding them from the bright day.

"I'm glad the clouds disappeared," she admitted as she popped the top of her grape-flavored beverage. "The sun came out for our first date. I take that as a good sign."

Kong reached under the table and pulled her feet onto his lap, then massaged her calf. "You look so fucking beautiful today."

"Funny, I've been checking you out, too. Now," she said in her best business voice, "I know almost everything about every regular in Sammy's bar, but I don't know near enough about you. Tell me your secrets."

Kong's sexy mouth bracketed with smile

lines when he grinned and poured barbecue sauce onto his sandwich. "I hung out at Sammy's over the years just so I could see you."

"You're teasing me."

He laughed and ducked the potato chip she threw at him. "I swear. I knew I couldn't be with you, but I needed to at least see you. When I tried to stop myself and go cold turkey on my Layla fix, my animal got hard to control."

"I looked forward to work because there was always the chance I would get to see you."

"No shit?" he asked, rubbing her calf again.

With a definitive nod, she said, "Zero shits."

Kong took a bite of his sandwich and looked off into the woods behind Moosey's. He gulped the food down and said, "Remember that guy who wouldn't stop grabbing your ass a few months back?"

"Yeah, the tourist with the crazy eyes. That guy was a jerk. Thankfully he only came in that one night."

"Because I followed him to the parking lot and just about knocked his eyes straight. Kirk had to pull me away before I really went to town, but I told the guy if he ever came back,

I'd know about it, and then I'd find him. I hated that he'd ruffled you. I know you can take care of yourself, and I've watched you put drunk assholes in their place so many times it's not even funny. But I passed the office on my way to the bathroom to get myself under control, and I heard you crying in there. It gutted me. I went after him the second he left."

She pursed her lips against the memory of that night. It had been one of the worst shifts she'd ever worked, and she hadn't known it at the time, but Kong was right there with her. "I think you were mine way before last week."

Kong licked his bottom lip and bit it as he nodded. "I've been yours for a long time."

She ate for a while in silence, absorbing that eye-opening morsel of information. "So next time I'm working, are you going to ignore me?"

"Hell no. I hated having to do that before. I don't have to do that anymore. I can even give you rides to and from your shifts if you ever want them. I close down the sawmill around six unless we have a big lumber order." Kong leaned forward, elbows on the table as he clasped his hands over his plate. "I like this."

"What?"

"Talking about our future. Of what our

future could be. It makes things...easier."

"What things?" she asked, confused.

His mouth twitched at the corner, and he relaxed back onto the picnic table bench. "This week has been brutal, and it's easy to get overwhelmed right now. Thinking about our future reminds me of what I'm fighting for. It makes anything seem possible."

"Okay," she said with a frown. "Christmas."

Kong grinned and tipped his head. "Easy. Spend them with the Gray Backs."

"The first person you'll call when we have our first baby."

"My mom. She's always wanted me to do this. It's why she left our family group with me when I was little. She wanted me to settle down and fall in love the way it felt right to me." Kong poked his sandwich with his plastic fork and slowed his words down. "She would like you. You're strong and independent, and you care about people in a way that inspires other people to be better. You put others above yourself." He looked up at her. "My mom is like that, too."

"Are you worried about her?"

He nodded slowly as he clasped his hands in front of his face. "Every action I take has a consequence for someone I love."

The sandwich she was munching on lost its flavor all the sudden and sat like a cold lump in her stomach. She pushed away the plate and reached across the table, rubbed her fingertips against his elbow.

Kong had said she was someone who put others above herself, but he didn't see the same value in himself. He'd been doing that since Fiona had broken him. He hadn't lived his life for himself at all. He hadn't approached Layla for years, even though he had wanted her. Kong had lived an empty, hollow existence to make life easier for other people.

Kong didn't see it, but she did.

He was the inspiring one.

FOURTEEN

"Put your bathing suit on, humaaan," Willa sang from behind an oversize pair of red sunglasses. She was holding an erotic romance book in one hand, a towel draped over her forearm, and in the other a beach bag that was almost as big as her.

"I didn't pack a bathing suit," Layla said from the rocking chair on 1010's porch.

"Well your big ol' teats aren't fitting in any of my extra small child-size tankinis. I'll ask Georgia and Gia if they have spares. BRB."

"BRB?" Kong asked through an amused smile.

"Be right back!" Willa called, her flip flops clacking loudly as she jogged away.

"Where are we going?" she asked Kong, who'd apparently already gotten the memo because he was wearing a pair of white swim trunks with a subtle, gray plaid print. His chest was bare, showing off all those scars she now found devastatingly sexy.

"We're taking you to the falls."

"The falls?"

"Bear Trap Falls, and you'll be one of the few humans to ever see it. The river splits the territory line between the Gray Backs and the Boarlanders. It's the best swimming hole in Damon's mountains, and you deserve a day to just have fun." His look darkened as he scanned the woods again. He did that a lot now. "We all deserve a break after the week we've had."

"Eee!" Layla squeaked, clenching her fists and waving them in tiny circles with uncontrolled excitement. "I love swimming, and I love waterfalls, and I've heard of Bear Trap Falls but never thought I would get to see it."

Kong laughed, hooked an arm around her waist, pulled her close, and pressed his lips against her forehead. "The water will be cold this early in the season, but we'll get used to it. The Gray Backs are doing a bonfire, so we'll spend the day there and just forget about everything, okay?"

"Did you set this up?" she asked.

His proud smile was answer enough. Her big, tough mate was also caring enough to offer her beautiful distractions.

"I'm the luckiest." Layla kissed his cheek and bounded into 1010 to gather sunscreen, sunglasses, towels, and the like. She had everything stuffed into her backpack by the time Willa danced in, swinging a purple bikini and gyrating her hips like a pole dancer. Layla giggled and danced around her, poking her fingers into the air and double-time tiptoeing across the semi squishy floors of 1010.

"So sexy," Kong teased from his spot leaning against the doorframe. An easy grin was splitting his face, and his dark eyes were dancing, exposing the happy, carefree side she'd only seen him have with the Gray Backs in Sammy's Bar when the Beck Brothers were playing a show. Today was going to be amazing.

"Okay, strap them udders into this and meet us outside," Willa said in a giddy voice. "Snap, snap, human. It was a long winter without Bear Trap Falls, and I have copious amounts of s'mores I need to shove into my mouth hole."

Layla dressed and slipped her feet into a pair of flip-flops, then followed Kong out of the trailer. He looked so cute with her pink, glittery backpack over his shoulder. Tan skin, muscles everywhere, and the man didn't mind glitter if it meant he could carry her stuff and take care of her. God, she loved him so much her heart felt like it was going to swell out of her chest.

"Aaah," she yelled as she ran for him and leapt onto his back. He didn't even buckle under her weight, just put his hand back behind him under her butt to keep her steady and kept walking.

"Sexy little monkey," he murmured with a smile in his tone.

"Oo oo, ah ah."

His laugh was booming and echoed through the trailer park. The sound of it sent a delicious shiver up her spine that landed in her shoulders, and she held on tighter around his neck, nuzzling her face against his warm skin.

She would have to go back to work again soon. Back to trying to catch up on bills. She would have to go back to Saratoga and face her old life and all the memories there, but for today, she didn't have to worry about anything. She just had to exist, and laugh, and enjoy every breath she had been blessed with because today was about taking a break from the muck. And as she grinned at the old white Chevy pickup with everyone piling in the bed around a giant cooler, she wouldn't have picked anyone else to spend the day with.

She had to sit on Kong's lap, but that didn't suck. And as Beaston drove them down an old washed-out road, she laughed along with the others at their easy banter. Oh, the Gray Backs might be notoriously broken bears, but she didn't see that from the inside. They were the warmest, most accepting batch of people she'd ever met. And they'd taken her right in when Kong had needed them to. She got it now. Kong had admitted that he wished he was a Gray Back, and watching them with their mates, laughing, joking, hugging and including her and Kong—always including them—she understood his desire to be a part of this.

They unloaded at a clearing in the woods. Ancient pines swayed this way and that in the breeze, creaking out Mother Nature's welcome. Waterlogged moss and vibrant green ferns made the woods look lush and alive. Kong gripped her waist and helped her over the edge of the pickup bed, then he pulled her arms around his neck again and carried her ape-style behind the others along a thin deer trail. She bit the back of his neck gently, then followed it with a soft kiss. The sound of running water and birds up in the canopy was so much more beautiful now that she knew how ugly life could be. This place was washing away the lingering hurt that had darkened her middle. Kong had been right. 1010 was magic, but so was this place.

She gasped as they crested the hill. The river was wide, but not too wide to swim all the way across if she was so inclined. On either side, towering evergreens lined the sandy bank. And up ahead, a huge waterfall was creating an ethereal looking mist as the river above them tumbled down against the water below. "I've never seen anything so lovely," she said on a stunned breath.

Kong gave her a sideways glance as he followed the others down toward a stretch of sandy bank. "Me either," he murmured.

Her middle turned warm and fuzzy as she held onto his neck tighter in a little hug that said without words that she adored him. Sweet mate. *Mate.* The thought still made her stomach do flip flops. It still took her breath away and made her feel like she was glowing. *The luckiest.*

Beaston and Creed set the giant blue

cooler in the sand, and in a matter of seconds, bag chairs were set up and beers were passed out. Kong declined one, though.

"What, are you pregnant?" Willa deadpanned with a frown.

"No," Kong said. "I just want to keep my head today."

Creed stared at him with the same slight frown and tight-eyed suspicious look Layla had been shooting at him the past couple of days. Creed noticed it too. Kong was still holding onto something she couldn't guess at. Secretive mate.

"I'll drink for the both of us," she offered, taking the crews' attention away from Kong.

"Yeah," Willa drawled, handing her a blue can. "I know you're not pregnant."

Not yet. Someday she would give Kong a baby, but not yet.

She raised her beer with the rest of them.

"C-team," the Gray Backs chanted.

"C-team," she murmured just a second later, baffled on where the toast came from. They weren't C-team to her. They were the finest, most caring people she'd ever had the pleasure of spending time with.

The Gray Backs were A-team.

"Last one in is a hairy monkey!" Willa

yelled pointing at Kong. She cackled and took off into the river, beer held high and sloshing.

Kong snorted and ran for the waves with the rest of them. All but Beaston and Aviana, who lowered baby Rowan to a blanket they'd spread out.

"You aren't swimming?" Layla asked the wild-eyed Beaston.

He cradled the baby gently in his lap and rocked back and forth. Never taking his eyes from Rowan's face, he said, "Creed said I could protect our little dragon today. Don't want to swim."

Aviana's black, shiny hair twitched as she cocked her head at her mate with a tender smile.

"Kong won't drink. I won't either. Not today." Beaston looked up at her with those clear, demon-bright green eyes. "We both have something important to protect. I have a gift for you." He leaned over and pulled a leather sheath from a canvas satchel beside him. He dipped his gaze back to Rowan, but held the fine leather sheath up to Layla.

"For me?" she asked, baffled. "What for?"

"Because girls like things that match."

"Oh." She took the knife and sat down beside Aviana, then unsnapped the clasp that held the blade into place and gripped the smooth wooden handle. When she unsheathed it, her heart stuttered at how fine the knife was. She didn't know much about them, but this looked to be very high quality, from the tapered edge of the blade to the polished silver that had a soft wave in color she'd never seen before. And etched onto the blade near the hilt was *K + L*.

Aviana leaned forward and pointed to the inscription. "All of the women in the Gray Backs have one just like it. Easton is very good at making knives. He made this one especially for you."

"K + L?"

"Kong and Layla," Beaston murmured, still rocking Rowan. "You're good to your bones. A good match. A love match. Not like with Kong's shit people."

Tears stung her eyes as she looked back down at the gift in her hands. "Thank you," she whispered. "This is the nicest gift anyone has ever given me."

Beaston nodded, looking pleased, and Aviana hugged her shoulders as Layla snapped the knife back into the sheath and tried to get her emotions under control. She'd sworn she wouldn't cry today, but two minutes on the sandy river bank, and a tear slipped down her cheek.

But this wasn't the sad kind she'd been leaking for Mac.

This was the happy kind, so it didn't count.

****

Kong sat by the fire, watching his mate laugh and splash around with Willa, Aviana, and Georgia in the middle of the river. The glow of the bonfire collided with the blue, full moonlight that danced across the dark water, illuminating her grinning, beautiful face.

Damn, today had been good for his animal. Watching Layla cut loose had settled some of his uncertainty. He would keep her safe no matter what. He had to. She was too important to this world for him to fail.

"You look like shit, man," Matt said with a grin, plopping down in the sand beside him and jerking his chin at Kong's mangled chest.

Kong huffed a laugh and looked pointedly at the crisscrossing scars that formed a spider web across Matt's entire torso. The scars he'd gotten from a government facility as a kid. "Now we match."

Matt fist bumped him and leaned back on his locked elbows, his eyes on Willa. "Twinsies," he muttered.

"Spill it," Creed said low as he dropped down in the sand on the other side of Kong. "You've been jumpy all week, and now you can't even have a beer? This isn't over, is it?"

Kong swallowed hard and shook his head, wishing with everything he was that his answer could be different.

"Why is Fiona obsessed with you?" Creed asked as he snapped a twig into small pieces.

"Because she's bad and needs to be cut down," Beaston said from Matt's other side as he watched Gia suckle Rowan at her breast. "Fiona is a bad tree. Rotten. Rotting all the trees around her." He swung that eerie, knowing gaze to Kong. "She wants to rot you, too."

Sometimes Beaston made more sense than anyone Kong had ever met.

"Fiona wants offspring from me," he said low so Layla wouldn't hear. "She's ready to breed."

"Barf," Matt muttered.

Kong huffed a surprised laugh. He really couldn't imagine bedding Fiona without his animal convincing him to strangle her.

Creed leaned back on his arms and stretched his legs in the sand. "So what's our play? Clearly she is going to come for you at some point."

Kong sifted sand through his hand and shook his head. "Not *our* play. *My* play. I can't put you at risk. This one is on me."

"And how do you see that working out?" Creed asked. "What is a realistic end result of going to war with your people alone?"

"Death," Beaston murmured.

"Death," Jason agreed from Beaston's other side.

Matt nodded slowly, eyes on the fire. "Death. For you and for Layla."

Kong gritted his teeth and inhaled deeply at the image of Layla lying in the field of red-stained wildflowers that had almost been his deathbed. "Creed, you have a family to protect."

"I do," he said somberly. Creed swung his dark gaze to Kong. "And you and Layla are a part of that now." He jerked his chin toward the girls who were bobbing on the waves, talking low and laughing with each other. "What kind of alpha would stand by while your people hurt Layla? Hmm? Losing Layla would hurt the rest of my crew now. And what kind of alpha would I be if I stood by and let you sacrifice yourself for your cause?"

"It's *my* cause—"

"Choosing your own mate is a just cause!" Creed barked out in a steely voice. "You don't belong with Fiona's people." He dragged his attention back to the waves, his jaw clenched in the flickering firelight. "You never really did."

FIFTEEN

Today had been an incredible respite from everything that had happened. Waterlogged, full of hot dogs and s'mores, and chilly from the late night breeze, Layla watched the Gray Backs filter into their trailers, chuckling softly and talking low as they disappeared.

She was sitting on the top stair of 1010's porch, legs splayed on either side of Kong where he sat a couple of stairs down. He was leaning back into her as he chewed languidly on a long piece of wild grass.

Layla wrapped her arms around his neck from behind and pressed her cheek against the back of his head. "You make me so happy."

Kong chuckled as he threw the grass away from him, then kissed her hand. He turned and opened his mouth to say something, but a limb snapped in the woods, and the words got caught in his throat. Kong jerked his head to the side, listening.

"What is it?" Layla asked, panic clawing through her.

"Go tell Creed they're here," he rumbled in an inhuman voice. When he turned, his eyes were hard and churning bright green. "Warn the others, then get inside and stay there."

"Kong, what's happening?"

"Fiona's here."

Fiona? She didn't understand. This was over. Over. Why was that horrible woman still after them? And why did Kong look completely unsurprised that she was here?

"What are you going to do?" she asked as he stood to his full height and pulled his shirt over his head.

He leaned down and kissed her on the forehead, then murmured, "What I should've done a long time ago."

He sauntered off toward the front of the trailer park, and Layla blasted off the porch and toward Creed and Gia's trailer. "Creed!"

The alpha was already coming down the steps of his trailer, pulling his shirt off. "I hear them. Matt! Jason!" He was punching something into his cell phone but he stopped to turn and yell, "Beaston!" off toward the tree line.

The Gray Backs trickled out, faces somber and ready. Gia came to stand by Layla with baby Rowan in her arms. "I think we should go inside."

"You go," Layla said drawing the knife that Easton had made her from its sheath on her hip. "This is because of me. I can't just hide and let Kong get hurt for me again."

A silver sedan pulled slowly up the gravel road. Its windows were tinted too dark to see inside but Layla would bet her life she knew who was driving. After the vehicle stopped, a slim woman in a dark business suit unfolded from the car. She stood ramrod straight, chin held high over a long, graceful neck as she looked down her nose at them in turn. Her chestnut brown hair was pulled so tightly into a curled updo, it looked headache inducing. She looked pale as the moon from the glow of outdoor lights that illuminated the trailer park. Her eyes were so light, they looked white, and were cold as death as she narrowed her inhuman gaze on Kong.

"Fiona," he greeted in a dead voice.

"You've caused us quite a mess of trouble, Kong, breaking your contract for a human *whore*." She clenched her fists and smiled thinly. Voice steadier, she continued. "And then you killed my best guards and made us come all the way up here to retrieve you."

"Us?" Kong gritted out.

Behind Fiona, the trees shook with dark figures, and giant gorillas appeared from behind the tree line on the forest floor, roaring and beating their chests. There had to be a hundred of them, at least.

Layla gasped as they approached closer from the shadows of the trees, the animals illuminated silver in the moonlight. Each was massive and thickly muscled as they exposed bright white canines that looked impossibly long and contrasted starkly against the dark knight.

On shaky legs, Layla weaved through the Gray Backs and stood next to Kong.

"Hi there," she said, meek as a mouse. Layla gripped the handle of her knife harder and anchored herself in the moment. In a stronger voice, she said, "Human whore here, and I'd just like to say—"

"You don't speak to me," Fiona said, eyes livid. "How dare you—"

"Shut the fuck up!" Layla yelled, fury blasting through her like a grenade. Red tinged everything. Red gorillas, red Fiona. "You are so desperate to keep Kong at your beck and call." She dragged her gaze across the gorillas inching closer out of the trees. "Are any of you happy? Are you? Are you so weak you would put a monster like Fiona on a pedestal and allow her to make all the decisions for your lives? How many of you has she broken? Huh? How many! Are you happy with the family groups she places you in, or do you wish you could choose your own? Do you wish it was about more than just some scientific chart that shoves you together regardless of your feelings? Regardless of your similar interests? Kong chose me. *Me*! He doesn't want to be with you, doesn't want to head a family group. He doesn't want to breed mindlessly. He's happy with me. And P.S.," she snapped at Fiona. "I tainted his seed, like, ten times already."

Fiona clenched her fists and crossed her arms. Her eyes blazed the color of snow, contrasting eerily with the darkness around her. "Bring her out."

The back door of her sedan opened, and a man emerged, dragging a shorter woman by the arm.

"Kong!" The woman screamed past a swollen, bloody lip. "Don't you dare give into them!"

Something powerful blasted through the air an instant before Kong lifted his arms into the air. His skin ripped apart, bones breaking as an enormous gorilla exploded from his skin. He slammed his closed fists onto the ground and shook the earth beneath her feet so hard Layla stumbled backward.

The man shoved the woman, Kong's mother, to the ground and gripped the back of her hair. A pained sound wrenched from her throat.

Beaston stepped forward beside Layla. "We sure do appreciate you bringing the mother of the Kong so we don't have to track her down."

"You'll watch her die," Fiona spat out. "Stupid silverback. You've just killed all of your little friends. Do you think I give a shit that you're surrounded by a handful of grizzlies right now? You're outnumbered a hundred to one!"

Layla panted in horror as she watched Kong's towering form pace in front of the Gray Backs, eyes on his mom. His massive shoulders flexed with each step he took, and his ebony lips pulled back to expose three inch long canines. He was bigger than the other gorillas by a head at least.

"Oooh, look at those pretty markings," Willa said as she approached Kong slowly. She jerked her chin. "Look at that gray back. You want to hear something terrifying about the Gray Backs?" Willa asked Fiona through a smile.

A long, prehistoric roar bellowed through the trees and shook the mountains. Birds flew from the evergreen canopy in droves, and the gorillas behind Fiona jumped, screamed, and stumbled backward.

Willa quirked her head. "Gray Backs fall under the protection of the last immortal dragon." She lifted her voice higher above the rising discord of the screaming, frantic gorillas behind Fiona. "As almost alpha of the Gray Backs—"

Creed sighed and corrected, "Second of the Gray Backs—"

"I claim Kong and his chosen family group as honorary members of this crew. So unless you want to be burned into crispy gorilla bacon and devoured by a grumpy dragon, I think you should release Momma Kong and kindly fuck off."

Fiona had the good sense to at least look nervous as she yelled, "Kill them all," behind her at the panicking gorillas.

Fiona's army shook the trees but didn't advance any closer.

"Perhaps you didn't understand her," Creed drawled out. "So I'll explain it like this. The Ashe Crew and the Boarlanders are charging through the woods right now, boxing you in. You have maybe two minutes before they're on you, and then the entirety of your fucked up shifter species will be dead. *Dead*, Fiona. All for a man who doesn't want you. He isn't Kong of the Lowlanders anymore. He's Kong of the Gray Backs."

The gorillas behind Fiona were melting back into the forest as Fiona screamed at them to, "Hold your ground!"

Now the woods echoed with the roaring of the bears.

"One minute," Creed said blandly. "What'll it be?"

An enormous figure flew overhead, blocking out the moon and bending trees under the powerful beat of its wings.

Beaston shook his head sympathetically beside Layla. "Mad dragon. Had to stitch our Kong back together. He's going to eat you. Chomp."

"Shut up," Fiona said, looking at the sky.

"Chomp," Beaston said again through a feral smile.

"I said shut up!"

The man who held Kong's mother released her and ran for the car.

"Run, little monkey," Beaston said.

"Never!" Fiona shrieked as her car backed away behind her. "You're mine! Mine! Do you hear me? I'll never rest until you are broken beneath me!"

Kong beat his chest and roared.

Kong's mother was running toward them at a dead sprint as Fiona's car sped away. Layla rushed forward and grabbed her hand. "Run," Layla urged Kong's mother. Panicked, she said, "Don't stop." Something awful was about to happen. Her instincts screamed to escape the clearing.

The Gray Backs were retreating with them now, too, sprinting toward the trailers as the breeze that had been a whisper moments before kicked up to gale-force. The sky went dark above them.

Terror clogged Layla's throat as something massive wrapped around her waist. Kong crushed Layla and his mother against his chest as they skidded to a stop on the dusty gravel road. Behind his massive shoulders, the night sky lit up with burning fire. *So hot. Hard to breath.* Tears streamed down Layla's face as she clutched the thick fur on Kong's arm.

A moment dragged on and on, and then suddenly, it was done.

The heat lifted, and the night was doused in darkness once again. All that was left of Fiona was a long streak of charred grass and billowing smoke.

A few feet away, Beaston hovered over Aviana, shielding her with his body. He dragged his inhuman gaze over the scorched earth and whispered, "Chomp."

SIXTEEN

"Barney, you're cut off," Layla said, taking his empty glass away to clean it.

"I'm barely tipsy," he argued.

Jake settled the phone into its sling and said, "Perfect timing because your brother is in the parking lot waiting for you."

"It's only eight."

"It's ten, and Sammy's has been booked for a private party."

Layla frowned at the back of her boss's head as he led Barney toward the door. "What private party?"

If Jake heard her, he ignored her like a champ. Not once did he turn around as he made his way to the door with a stumbling Barney. A stream of customers flooded in around them, and a grin split her face when she saw Willa and Aviana at the helm.

"Mid-week and the Gray Backs are here? Party animals," Layla teased as she wiped down the sticky bar top where Barney had spilled half his last drink.

"We need tons of shots," Willa said as she sat on the barstool.

"What's the occasion?" she asked.

Willa jerked her head toward the door just as Kong ducked under the frame. "You."

With an uncertain smile, she shook her head, baffled. "Okay, how many shots is a ton?"

Denison and Brighton were now up on stage plugging in their cables, and the rest of the Ashe Crew were trickling in around Kong.

"Enough shots for all the crews and Damon," Willa said.

Layla's eyes nearly bugged out of her head. "Damon is going to be here?" As far as she remembered, the gorilla-chomping dragon had never set foot in Sammy's Bar.

Aviana leaned over, her eyes bright and excited. "Rumor has it he's coming down from his mountains to party with us."

Layla blinked hard and whispered, "Wow," as she began lining up all the clean shot glasses they had.

Layla laughed and chatted as her friends dropped by the bar to say hello. Maybe this was a version of the Shifter Nights she and Jake had discussed. If so, he could've warned her, though. She went from a few customers to slammed in seconds. Jake helped her rush to fill glasses, and every time she looked up, Kong was watching her with such adoration in his gaze. He didn't have to ignore her anymore. One of many changes that had happened in the two months since Fiona's barbecue.

Now, Kong's mother, Josephine, and Kirk helped him run the sawmill. Layla had wiggled out of her apartment lease and had moved into Kong's cabin with the three of them. It was crowded, but anyone with eyes could see it was good for Kong to live near Kirk and Josephine. Layla smiled as happy warmth flooded her cheeks. Kong had the best of both worlds now, as he deserved. He was a part of the Gray Back Crew, and he'd secured a family group in Saratoga.

And Fiona would never hurt them again.

Layla called out, "Pass 'em around!" and laughed as she watched the most important people in her life hand out shots through the notes of the Beck Brothers' song. Her eyes landed on Kong as he wove through the crowd and approached the bar.

His eyes were soft brown and locked on

hers. Tall, strong, scarred, and with that hesitant smile tugging at his lips, Layla's breath froze in her chest with how beautiful he was. When he reached the bar, he set a book on top of it.

She read the title. *Heart in the Riptide*. It was the last book she'd read to Mac before he died. Layla shook her head, confused.

"Shh!" Willa and some of the others hissed. The shifters settled, and the room went silent except for the soft notes Denison and Brighton played on their guitars.

Kong licked his lips, then lifted his voice. "I only got to meet Mac one time. He made me read this book to him, but near the end of Chapter Sixteen, I couldn't do it anymore. It hit too close to home. And before I left, he told me that someday, I should read the end of the book."

Layla bit her trembling lip as her eyes filled with tears. She remembered how the book ended.

Kong pushed the book across the bar top and smiled, his eyes full of emotion.

"Read it!" Creed called across the bar.

"Read it," the others said.

Layla huffed a thick laugh and nodded. "Okay."

A few cheered and a few whistled as Kong opened it to the last page of Chapter Sixteen. Wiping her damp lashes to clear her vision, Layla cleared her throat and read. "So many decisions in his life that got him to this exact moment in time would haunt him, but he couldn't regret the journey. The jagged road he'd taken in his life had led him to a few glorious moments with her. He'd lived more in the last two weeks than he had in the entirety of his forgettable life because he'd known love—the bone-deep kind that changed a man from the inside out. And now…he knew sacrifice. The riptide carried her farther and farther, the strokes of his first mate's oars like a lash against his heart every time they dragged through the choppy water. Was this really what sacrifice meant? He couldn't breathe, couldn't take his eyes away from his love as she wept silently, eyes filled with tears that he'd caused. Sacrifice wasn't supposed to hurt them both this much. He had a responsibility to the ship, to the crew, but none of that seemed to matter when he could see he was ripping her heart out by sending her away. It didn't matter to his love that he was trying to keep her safe from the dark end that awaited every pirate. It only mattered that they would be separated from here on. For the rest of their lives, they would bear a hole in them that was too deep to ever be filled by another. He'd ripped that into her by allowing her to fall in love with him. He'd ripped it into himself by adoring her like this. As he stepped up to the railing and stared through the sea spray waves that pounded against his ship, he realized he'd had it all wrong. He wasn't supposed to give *her* up. He was supposed to give himself up. He turned and looked at his boat—the boat he'd worked his whole life to captain. He looked at his crew, and in their eyes, he could already see it—their silent goodbye. Standing on the bow, he inhaled the salty brine and closed his eyes against the sea mist, savoring it for the last time. Then he lifted his hands above his head and dove into the frigid, unforgiving waters below. Every stroke he swam toward his love changed him. Whoever he'd been yesterday didn't matter anymore. She required and deserved more. The only version of himself that mattered was the man he would be tomorrow—for her. And when he broke the surface to gulp air, she was there, tears glistening in her eyes and arms outstretched, ready to help him up. Ready to catch him.

Ready to push him to be the man she believed he could be." A tear slipped to Layla's cheek as she looked up at Kong and uttered the last lines. "She was everything, and he was nothing, and the sacrifice was never his to give. It was hers."

Layla blew a long, steadying exhalation of air as she wiped the tears from her face.

"Turn the page," Kong whispered.

She sniffed and turned the heavy paper slowly. On the other side was taped a simple white gold band and a key. Her face crumpled, and her vision blurred again as she plucked away the chipped, pink camouflage key she'd carried on her keychain since she was sixteen, up until the day she was asked to give it back to the bank that took Mac's house after his death.

"Did you buy Mac's house?"

Kong angled his head and nodded once.

"For me?"

He shook his head. "For us."

She laughed thickly as she pulled the ring off the back page. "Is this one for me?"

Kong leaned over the bar and kissed her softly. Just a sweet sip of her lips that said he loved her. Then he rested his cheek on hers and whispered against her ear, "Will you be mine?"

She gripped the back of his neck to keep him there against her, touching her until she could steady her thoughts enough to speak. She looked out at the Gray Backs and the Ashe Crew. At the Boarlanders and at Damon, who stood just on the outskirts of the shifters he protected. She'd always feared that when Mac died, she would be left alone in this world. No home, no purpose, no family.

She'd been so wrong.

As she dragged her gaze over her beloved Gray Backs to Josephine, who smiled through her tears beside Kirk, Layla drew a deep, steadying breath.

With a smile, she nuzzled her cheek against Kong's and whispered, "I've always been yours."

Want More of These Characters?

Try T. S. Joyce's Bestselling Saw Bears Series.

The Complete Series is Available Now

Lumberjack Werebear
(Saw Bears, Book 1)

About the Author

T.S. Joyce is devoted to bringing hot shifter romances to readers. Hungry alpha males are her calling card, and the wilder the men, the more she'll make them pour their hearts out. She werebear swears there'll be no swooning heroines in her books. It takes tough-as-nails women to handle her shifters.

Experienced at handling an alpha male of her own, she lives in a tiny town, outside of a tiny city, and devotes her life to writing big stories. Foodie, wolf whisperer, ninja, thief of tiny bottles of awesome smelling hotel shampoo, nap connoisseur, movie fanatic, and zombie slayer, and most of this bio is true.

Bear Shifters? Check
Smoldering Alpha Hotness? Double Check
Sexy Scenes? Fasten up your girdles, ladies and gents, it's gonna to be a wild ride.

For more information on T. S. Joyce's work,
visit her website at
www.tsjoycewrites.wordpress.com

Made in United States
Orlando, FL
03 May 2023